SISTERHOOD

THE NOVEL

Celebrating the ripples people leave behind...

Jolie

25th Jan 2020

SISTERHOOD
THE NOVEL

by

Jolie Booth

SISTERHOOD THE NOVEL
is typeset in
Book Antiqua, Castellar and Frankin Gothic
and published by
Kriya Arts, Marlborough Theatre,
4 Prince's Street, Brighton, BN2 1RD

Printed and bound in Great Britain by Amazon

Dedicated to all my sisters…

With special thanks to Arts Council England, Andrea Brooks, Caragh Rose-Bailey, Coco Maertens, Jules Craig, Sophia Craig-Daffern, Jamie-Rae Tanner, Alberta Jones, Jess Bernberg, Daisy Fitzsimmons, Sam Chittenden, Mish Maudsley, Lisa Lister… And the rest of the Sisterhood Coven

(That includes you)

PREFACE

Come now come now, each woman & girl,
Take your courage, as the flames, they curl,
We may burn at the hands of some men,
But from that fire we shall rise again.

I will follow my sisters three,
And sing upon the face of fear,
Our bodies they may burn and beat,
But this phoenix they shall never defeat.

PRELUDE

The next morning, they came for us.
The men…
Men we knew well.
Men we had seen grow up through boyhood from babes.
Men we had loved.
Some we had snatched kisses from beneath the greenwood tree. Some had been friends and brethren. Every word we'd ever said to them, now a rope around our necks.
Some had been beastly towards us before and it were no surprise to see their faces, black with intent, behind the door that morn. Some of them had already beaten us. Spat cruel words. Touched us in ways that were not right. Some had already taken us against our will.
They had all silenced us in their ways.
But the worst thing about that morn, it was not the men. We had expected them. We knew they would be behind the door when finally, it swung open. It was not their faces that broke our hearts.
It was the women…

Women we had helped.
Who we had bathed, birthed, tended to in their sickness and delivered their babes.
Women we had shown politeness to… And those we had not. Their faces were not black. Their faces were full of vengeance. Every slight. Every wrong that had ever been committed against them, which of course had been many, took pleasure in knowing that their revenge now had a place to reside. And it were in our pain, in our torture, in our humiliation and our deaths that they would find their release. For they would watch us swing with glee… If we were ever to make it that far.
They rubbed their hands as their eyes fell upon us. We saw their faces, as the light spilled in and caught our shaking forms squatting in the darkness at the back of the church. As if there were any refuge…
Out of all we had endured and all that now lay before us, it were that, their part in it and their delight in it, which hurt the most.

BELTANE

It is Beltane. Huzzah!

And I… SHE… Earth, am in love! Darlings… I'm in love! The air positively tinkles with my joy. Having given birth back at Imbolc to a sparkling beautiful young boy, after being so desperately sad that his father, the Sun, had died last Samhain and left me here heartbroken and alone… Still, I carried on regardless (I mean, what else is one meant to do?) through the long, dark and lonely winter months, growing the babe in my cauldron of power, my magnificent womb, enduring the sadness of isolation and my desperate mourning. Then, on February 1st, my baby was born… An Aquarius! And the boy I gave birth to, he was the most beautiful creature this universe had ever seen (according to me, which is a mother's prerogative). He was spritely and rambunctious. He had little cloven hooves and tiny little buds on his forehead that would one day grow to be magnificent antlers. He skipped and bounced about all over the newly blossoming landscape… And he grew, and he grew, and he grew. And he grew strong… And handsome; headstrong, independent, progressive and original. He had the most cheeky, lopsided grin, foppish blonde hair, sparkling green eyes, a lascivious laugh and all-over naughty disposition. And now he is a young man, with a swagger in his stride, broad shoulders, a rippling chest, shapely strong forearms and a fine pair of antlers. His musky odour smells like rutting sex. And of course, I also shed my skin with his birth and returned to my maiden state, so the smell of him is driving me utterly wild. My legs swish together with light translucent goo whenever he comes anywhere near me, or even just at the thought of him. If I hear him playing his pipes up on the hills, then I positively squeal with delight. He fills my every waking second. I love him! And he is utterly worthy of my love. We are made for each other. Everything of me, the EARTH, grows towards HIM, the light… The SUN!

And so also does everything in my dominion… In Wilmington, East Sussex, the Yew Tree sheds her skin too, splitting her trunk open suggestively to reveal fresh smooth bark beneath, as she shimmers dangerous outstretched needles towards her true love… The Longman on the Hill. Etched into the side of the downs, north side, so onlookers face his radiance, he shines back at her; newly chalked white for the day's festivities. For he is Belenus, the Sun God, the 'Fair shining one' and today we are celebrating HIM…

The bee flies from bloom to bloom; ravenous after his long slumber. The seductive flowers flaunt their stamens with delicious passages, beckoning in bees with promises of sweet and sticky pollen. Their vivid colours and scents heady with possibility, intoxicating every hungry beastie. Carpets of bluebells shimmer in chiffon drapes across the forest floor, heavy in dusty perfume and glistening in waves of lilac and cobalt blue, edged with puffs of Queen Anne's Lace. The smell of wild garlic catches on the nose beneath the shadier canopies, as the air pricks to the shrill beats of fresh chiffchaffs, welcoming home summer visitors, returning on the wing.

The jackdaw caws in satisfaction at his choice of chimney stack, within which he's begun to build this year's nest. He shouts his boastations, like a fifty-a-day smoker. Prancing lambs bleat excitedly in the fields; desperately seeking lost mothers, who call back loud but nonchalant, heavy from their grazing spots, the fields now lush green and healed from the muddy brown of winter spoil.

Pairs of brimstones and cabbage whites flutter by, dancing in twists and turns about the breeze; welcoming in the merry month of May. The cuckoo sings, the dragonfly takes his first flight and the hedgehog wakes. All are about their business.

Once more I have given birth to a multitude of little lives. Brothers and sisters scatter across the land, each with their own needs and desires, all intertwined. Every year is different, yet every year is the same. Everything is connected. Thousands upon thousands of turns of the wheel spiral onwards in a cycle of seasons, creaking forwards in progression, towards what will eventually be our ultimate demise. I have no favourites. I am fair in all. For I am the great MOTHER. You are all given the same serving under my dominion… You are all given a life.

DAY

Kitty woke to the bright golden light of Beltane pouring in as shimmering beams through the holes of her wooden shutters. She loved watching the dust play in the rays of light, like faery folk swinging about in midsummer madness. The sun spilled golden pools of heat across the bare floorboards, warming it readily for her dainty pale feet.

Then she thought of her feet… And how they would not be looking particularly dainty that morn. They were covered in mud, and dried on bits of grass, from where she had snuck out of the house in the early hours.

Lifting the covers to check the sheets, Kitty squealed in horror as she saw the mess at the bottom of her bed and quickly set about sweeping out dried mud and foliage. But it was too late. The sheets were smeared with stains. She had been too cold and frozen the night before to care about such things, leaping back into bed shivering. Now though, in the warmth of broad daylight, she knew her chambermaid Joan would suspect immediately that she had sneaked out of the house again. Kitty began to panic.

Throwing back the heavy woollen blankets and white linen sheets, she set about rubbing the fabrics together to remove the guilty marks of dried-on dirt, dusting off all the evidence from the side of her large four-poster bed. Once she felt she had rubbed the sheets sufficiently clean and could comfortably persuade all that the level of muck remaining was nothing more than what an average pair of grubby feet would leave, she lowered herself down from the huge oak bed and swept up all the debris from the floorboards.

Tip toeing over to the window, Kitty quietly opened the latches, pushing open the wooden shutters and swinging out the lead diamond windows. Blinking into the morning sun, she cast the evidence out onto the fresh spring breeze.

∞

Alice had been up since before dawn and was almost finished at the dairy, when the first blue light of morn began to creep up over Windover Hill. She had been working hard churning butter and cutting curds in time for full sunrise. It was all well and good folks only working half days on festive days, but that didn't stop the villagers wanting fat and cheese for their bread.

Her husband John had also been up since before the dawn, but then there was nothing unusual about this, what with him being a baker and all. He always rose whilst the moon was high in the night sky. Someone must knead the loaves and get them into the oven; baked, warm and ready for daybreak, when the rest of the villagers roused.

Alice had often pondered on whether John's late hours had born any influence on their difficulties, but the priest had been clear that if fault lay at anyone's feet, then it will be laid at those of Alice.

They'd laid together upon the yester, before he had left for the Bake house, for it be forbidden for them to lay together on Beltane eve, with it being a feasting day and all. Last night had been the closest Alice could get to being with her fellow on Beltane. She had coaxed him to his climax, before they slept, and he brought her to her pleasure too, so her womb had been made soft and fertile like freshly tilled soil, all ripe and ready for his seed, safely laying now in her belly, ready for jumping over the Beltane fires.

Lightly placing her white dairymaid's hand on the woollen dress, hanging loosely over her stomach, she breathed deeply into her womb, and willed the union to be fruitful.

∞

Marjorie let out a long and hearty fart as she bent over the bubbling pot of porridge hanging from an iron spit in her hearth. The hovel was squalid, but it be the way she liked it. And there was something captivating about the chaos of drying herbs; pots filled with curiosities and the huge variety of unusual utensils that hung from every possible space on the beams and filled every dusty corner. Scouring the teaming shelves and with furtive glances into the deep recesses of the sloping walls, one could see she was a mistress who had lived a long and interesting life.

The hovel was just a thatched roof that reached all the way down to the floor, boxed in at each end with wattle and daub walls, both ends bearing a simple door and glassless window. The hovel was filled with animals. Some, like the goats and chickens, clambered about in the rafters and were for sustenance. Some, like the cats and the little yapping mongrel, were for a spot of company, though they too fulfilled their uses as rat catchers, mousers and guards for the hovel. Marjorie did not appreciate freeloaders.

She had got up to watch the dawn rise and had collected a whole bottle of morning dew. She was now setting about breaking her fast before heading into the village, where she'd go about her daily business. With it being Beltane, she had plans for the eve, so it was to be a long and busy day. She was not as spritely as she'd used to be. Marjorie had reached sixty summers in March and was one of only four people in the village who had reached such an age. She must give herself plenty of time these days, to finish all that she had to do.

The first of which? Porridge.

∞

I wake up at my Mum's house, with the sun burning my face through the window. I'm parched and my mouth is furry. Flapping my hand wildly around the side of the bed, looking for water, I knock my charging phone to the floor. Cursing into the air, I find the pint glass, grab it and glug down a full pint; spilling liquid all over my chin and onto my already sweaty pillow.

Taking a quick glance at the space next to me, I'm relieved to see my bed is empty. The sun is super bright through the pale curtains, and I'm seriously unhappy about the fact, so start to look for something, *anything* to shield my eyes. Nearly pulling the bedside drawer from its rung, I dig around in the disarray until I find my eye mask with "Fuck off" emblazoned across the front in hot pink embroidery. I pull it over my face, pushing my short-cropped hair out of my eyes, and fall face first back onto the soggy pillow, letting out a long and tuneful moan.

∞

The golden light of May Day diffuses itself through the thin muslin curtains into the white-washed double bedroom where I am lying, curled up on Egyptian cotton sheets, next to my snoring husband. May Day is my favourite day of the year. So full of possibility for the coming summer, and today we'll be heading into town to watch the May Day celebrations in Queen's Park. Every year, for five years now, a company of artists have erected a May Pole in the park and there's been music and dancing and performances of old plays, like George and the Dragon. And everyone drinks ale and mead, whilst scoffing down a hog roast. The performers are always covered in green and crown their heads with flower garlands. I LOVE IT.

I go every year with my husband and another couple; close friends of ours who also love the festivities and who are also struggling to have children. We normally drink bubbles together and make our own garlands from flowers in the garden.

They will be arriving at our house in an hour, so I must begin the tiresome task of trying to get my husband roused and out of bed, ready in time for their arrival.

Swinging my legs down the side of the bed, I put on my sheepskin loafers and plod heavily down the wooden stairs to the kitchen. My weight has ballooned since I hyper stimulated from our last round of IVF.

It nearly killed me, and now I'm two stone heavier than I was before. This whole experience has been a fresh kind of hell.

Reaching the kitchen, I flick on the kettle and clean out the cafetière, ready to brew up some extra-strong coffee. I think about my husband and how hot and skinny he used to be. I would say we have both let ourselves go. But I try to watch what I eat and exercise all the time. Whereas he eats all the crap in the universe and has never seen the inside of a gym in his life. Looking at the way men treat their bodies, no wonder the world is fucked.

∞

Drinking nettle tea at my table beside the window, I look over towards the florist on the bustling street below and watch as a new palette of tulips arrive. I make a mental note to bring a bunch upstairs before setting out for the day. Miniature daffodils are already in full bloom on my kitchen table, but one can never have too many flowers in the house, now can one?

It has been a tough month. My mother has just had open heart surgery and I've been nursing her. Her heart calcified. My mother is quite literally hard-hearted. She has been rather amiable these last few weeks, which has made the whole process much easier, but I cannot forget, and must honour the truth that she has been my abuser for my entire life. I'm doing the right thing by her because I'm not an arsehole. But I must not forget myself and my truth in all of this.

Today is for me. The first day I have had to myself in weeks. I've lots of plans; one of which includes visiting Tom's grave. I'll take a tulip with me for that. And then I'll spend the afternoon with my goddaughter and her little ones. That's after a quick trip to the dentist. I did try to make the emergency appointment for another day, so as not to ruin an otherwise perfect afternoon, but the next slot hadn't been for a fortnight and my tooth is hurting awfully. I've chewed as many cloves as I'm going to get away with and the time has come to get the blasted thing sorted. My dentist is a lovely Kuwaiti woman who is kind and gentle, thank the heavens. It has taken me years to find a dentist I can trust. For some reason they have always freaked me out. I've had some brutes in my time, but the phobia seems to come from before any bad experiences that I can recall. I've never liked anyone going near my mouth, but I don't know why. As chance would have it, I discovered my fabulous new dentist at a practice just on the end of my street. I loved her instantly because she had total patience with me and my unreasonable terror. She even told me it was a common trait.

"My own mother is terrified of dentists," she'd said to me.

I responded, "Well you're the lucky one… Most dentists are terrified of my mother."

∞

Looking out the window, Kitty caught sight of the festivities assembling at the village green, down the lane, in front of the inn. Ribbons had been attached to the pole two days hence, but now they were being pinned out in a wide circle by several maids, whilst a group of fellows carried barrels of ale from the inn, out to the side of the green, where they would have time to sit and settle before the Beltane festivities began.

Each year, three respected men from the village were appointed Masters of the Green. Their station for the day; to protect the

Maypole from younger fellows of the neighbouring hamlets, who tried every year to steal the pole. They also had to oversee the general arrangements and man the barrels during church service, guarding them from the onslaught of greedy gullets. Mayhap the Masters of the Green would partake in a few short drafts themselves, it was hot work after all, but at least less ale would be drained by them than if the commoners got hold of it. That is what they liked to tell themselves anyway.

This Beltane, Kitty's father had been asked by the parish to fulfil this honour. He was asked most years. Kitty could see him now in his finest black silk suit, with that ridiculously large cod piece he was so fond of. It was all the rage at Henry's court apparently. The fashions of the city enthralled him, and he tried to force Kitty and her sisters to follow suit; gifting them dresses every time he returned from his travels. They made Kitty look foolish to the other villagers, whom she had to live amongst. She believed this is one of the main reasons why nobody liked her.

∞

Alice scrubbed the board clean and began to set it ready for the simple feast she would share with her husband later that day, after church had finished. They'd break their fast together, as was custom, with a little bread and cheese. Then they would douse their fire, ready for relighting with the new Beltane flame taken back to their cottage from the green. They would also partake in hog's flesh and sweet meats at the feast, so Alice wished not to fill their stomachs with their usual plain food. Her good man John was at the village green already, helping the other fellows lift and carry. She would meet him at the church.

Once the board was washed and dried, Alice looked out of the front window to the street... Folks from the village were going to and fro, bustling about their business, but none she could see had business with her, so quickly she removed some stowed away items that were hidden in the depths of her hanging pockets, and placed a quill, ink, clay bowl, wax and a seal upon the board. Alice gently extracted a piece of white cheese cloth from another pocket and unwrapped a pale blue chicken egg. Pulling a pin from her bodice, she held her intention of bearing a child in her mind before piercing the top of the shell. Turning the delicate egg about, she did the same again, before piercing the shell on the other side, so that she could then blow the contents into the bowl. Alice wiped the empty shell clean with her cheese cloth, took the quill, and etched symbols onto the smooth surface, like the ones the wise woman had shown her. Blowing the ink dry, she sealed one end with wax and pressed her husband's seal upon it. Then blowing into the egg once more at the open end, she captured her breath within the shell, before sealing it, also with the wax and seal. Finally, she whispered her prayer over the speckled blue surface and tapped it three times. She quickly cleared away the evidence, wrapping the charm safely back up in her cheese cloth, and stowing it gently away in her hanging pocket.

∞

Finishing a bowl of porridge, Marjorie sat back on her stool, let out a large belch, and snapped off the top of a willow from a half-woven basket on the floor beside her, absentmindedly using it as a toothpick. Satiated, she scoured the room and considered what job to do first... Mistress

Anne was due a visit as her poultice needed changing and Mistress Abys would need checking up on, to see how the babe was faring. Marjorie delivered the woman's baby two weeks hence - a daughter - and the babe had taken to the breast straightaway; but the child was the woman's first and her own mother had done little to guide her in the ways of such things. The mother had remarried when her first husband, the father of Mistress Abys, had died and she'd moved over to Brighthelmstone to start a second family, leaving poor Abys to fend for herself. Marjorie had already set her mind to take the ingredients she needed for a hot posset that would help to keep the milk flowing.

A cat jumped up onto Marjorie's lap, disrupting her from her musings and she stroked his matted fur, as he licked the porridge bowl clean, purring with contentment.

"Thou old scrag puss" rasped Marjorie, humouring him for a moment before batting him away with the back of her hand, shewing him from the table and back down onto the floor.

"I have no time for this scrag puss. Some folks have places to be."

With a loud groan, Marjorie slapped her hands down onto her thighs and raised herself stoically to her feet, making chickens scatter and squawk in excitement. She took her bowl and plunged it into the newly boiling cauldron of hot water that was hanging bubbling over the fire. With a scouring brush and lime soap, Marjorie scrubbed the utensils clean.

∞

"Carrie! Carrie! CARRIE!"

Mum is shouting at me… I pat around the ground by my bedside table, until finally I manage to fish up the phone by its charging lead. I pull up my mask, peer at the lit-up screen and groan. It's 10am. I drop the phone back to the floor with a thud, roll over and flop my arms above my head. I've got to be at Starbucks by 11.30am for my shift and I'm hungover as fuck. I reach out for more water, remembering I've already finished it, and so with the heavy sigh of a worker who hates their job, I pull the phone up by the charging lead again and start thumbing Facebook. Scrolling through the posts; liking, loving, wowing and dropping angry faces in my wake, I suddenly stop on a post by my little bro. He's posted photos of him out and about last night with a gang of mates I've never seen before, pushing each other around in shopping trolleys, being little shits by the looks of things, and it also appears they set fire to something. My stomach lurches. When I saw him yesterday, he'd asked me to lend him a tenner, for dog food he'd said, and I'd swore it was the last time I would ever lend him money again, unless he sorted his shit out. The tenner clearly didn't go on dog food. My fury gives me the energy I need to fight gravity and sit upright in bed.

The room begins to spin. Clothes and plates of half eaten food are strewn everywhere and the contents of my bag are spilled across the floor. I honestly can't remember getting home last night. I remember the pub closing at 1am… I'd gone back to some student house with my mates, Matt and Em, for a little night cap. We'd bought some take-outs and Em had pulled a couple of bags of speed out of his wallet. That was the last thing I remember.

Rifling back through my drawer, I sift through the shit to find my meds; half popped packs of fluoxetine, clozapine and trazodone. I suffer from anxiety attacks, and big bouts of depression… Fun. Cracking open the packets I pop the pills into the palm of my hand, give them their obligatory jiggle, and place them next to my empty pint glass. Right then, let me try and get my shit together…

∞

I open the backdoor and step out into the garden. The sun is shining, and the garden buzzes with the sound of bees. I love this garden. It's an old woman's garden. In fact, it really was the garden of an old woman, who used to live here before us, and died here too, before we took up our tenancy. She'd evidently lived in this house a long time, due to the lack of central heating and the crazy 1980's décor. She'd also clearly loved this garden. And now I love it too. I didn't touch it for a year, wanting to see what would grow if left to its own devices. Then this year, having decided a whole flower bed of geraniums was probably unnecessary, I dug up half and filled it with meadow flowers. Despite the cats thinking this freshly tilled soil was their new giant litter tray, a good crop of colourful and delicate flowers still managed to emerge. And it is these little beauties that are attracting all the bees, just as I had hoped they would.

My husband is thankfully up and about. He's in the kitchen, cooking scrambled eggs, and our friends will be over shortly. I'm showered and dressed, wearing a summery floral frock, though I still need a pair of leggings under my dress and a cardigan covering my bare arms, to keep me warm. The sun is hot, but the air is still fresh from winter.

I'm trying to decide which flowers to cut for our garlands, but my dress keeps catching on the tiny wounds across my belly, distracting me from the task at hand. Pulling up my frock, I examine my stomach and let out a little whimper. It is black and blue with bruises and covered in little red pin pricks from all the injections. We are halfway through our third and final round of IVF, with another 10 days to go until the trigger injection and egg harvesting operation. It's our final round, because this is the last attempt we'll get for free on the NHS and neither of us earn enough money to fork out £10,000 a pop to try again after this.

I'll be drinking no mead or bubbles at the May Day celebrations this year. But hopefully, next year, I'll be taking my newborn baby along to the fun.

∞

I clear away the breakfast things from my little wooden butterfly table and place the cut glass vase of vivid red tulips next to my window casement.

"You are too excitable" I scold them and pluck one from the bunch to take to Tom's grave. It's not actually a grave, as in the place where he is buried. Tom was cremated and his ashes separated into multiple little transparent drug baggies. These were handed out to his nearest and dearest with separate A4 sheets explaining where to pour the contents of each bag, the instructions guiding them to places where he'd remembered spending special times with them. I had been given three bags; one for my old basement flat, where he'd often turned up unexpectedly over the years, at all the ungodly hours, pissed out of his head. Another one was for the pub we'd frequented the most over the years. The last one was for the bench where we would sit when we went on our walks. It looks out over the sea from the top of Saltdean cliffs. It is this bench that I think of as his grave and is where I go when I want to spend time with him. The baggy of ashes meant for my flat came with me to my new place when I moved a couple of years ago.

A new top floor one-bedroom flat that's filled with sunshine and looks out over one of the busiest bustling streets in the bohemian quarter of the city centre. My last place had been renovated and all the tenants thrown out, even though I'd lived there for over ten years. It had been my home and I was heartbroken at the time. But it had all turned out for the best, because it had not occurred to me until I'd moved, how much the light (or lack of) had been affecting my mood and that the incessant damp had been impacting my health. The new flat I live in now is divine and filled with a lifetime's worth of charming and meaningful objects, because I brought them with me.

∞

Kitty had three younger sisters, but from her father's second wife. Kitty's mother had died in childbirth. Her mother had been convinced that Kitty was a boy, before she had been born, so when her mother had seen Kitty was in fact a girl, it had killed her. Or so Kitty's father had told her. He'd remarried 8 years later, and the younger sisters had been raised to dislike Kitty by her conniving stepmother, who was hell bent on convincing her father to cut Kitty from his will. She'd intended to marry Kitty off as soon as possible, to get her out of the way, and had nearly managed to send Kitty packing to the home of an awful fellow, who was older than her father, when Kitty had been but twelve summers old. The deal had almost been sealed, when Kitty's stepmother suddenly fell ill with the pox and died. Kitty's father found he needed a woman, someone to run the house and raise the younger girls. This responsibility fell to Kitty. She now had to tend to three younger sisters who did not like her and hardly spoke to her, whilst also tending to a grieving father who wished she was a boy. He increasingly kept away on ever longer voyages. Kitty had twenty summers now, and the offer of marriage still stood from the fowl old man she had been betrothed to. Her father would be forced to soon begin the arrangements. He did not want to be left with a spinster to look after and the sisters were old enough now to care for themselves with the help of the maids. Kitty knew it would be likely they'd be wedded by this time next year. This was the reason Kitty felt perpetually sick and unable to sleep at night. One of the reasons, anyway.

∞

Taking the bowl of raw egg, Alice walked into the kitchen feeling a huge sense of relief. This had been the first time she had ever done anything like this before and her blood was beating hard against her skull. Taking some bound willow sticks, she whisked the eggs and mixed in ingredients to make biscots, adding cinnamon to the bowl, as the wise woman had also advised. Whilst beating the mixture, Alice muttered her prayer again under her breath, beating away until she had made a dough. She rolled the ball out into a long worm, cut it into two pieces and weaved both pieces into knots. She placed them on the hot bricks inside her fireplace, cleaned herself up, and went to her bed chamber to change for church.

∞

Along the path to Mistress Anne's house, Marjorie saw that the wild garlic was out and stopped to pick a great quantity of leaves, piling them into her basket. Blossoms blew from the trees around her, giving the impression of snow. The banks were lined with primroses, bluebells and daffodils. In the field beyond the hedgerow, lambs bleated in terror as farmers went about checking them, to see they were fit and healthy. Their mothers returned their calls with their own panicked bleats. Today the farmers would be driving their cattle out into the fields, so they needed to check their flocks were all in prime condition before setting them to pasture.

Bees buzzed and the air tinkled with sweet seductive anticipation. Marjorie hummed to herself as she made up two little posies of yellow flowers and placed them in her basket; gifts for the women she would be visiting that day. Continuing up the path, she noted that a great quantity of flowers had already been picked and guessed these would have been for the May Queen's garland, or to dress the cattle and the well. Marjorie was very fond of the well dressing. She once saw Our Lady appear to her down at that blessed well, and she knew Our Lady was fond of spring flowers, so she hoped she might catch sight of her again today.

∞

The shower helped. A little. Wrapped in a towel, I sniff at my clothes in turn to see which ones are clean enough for work. My uniform t-shirt is crumpled as fuck, so before I dry my hair, I put it on and blast the inside with my mum's hairdryer. I turn my attention to my hair; scrunching it about, moving it from side to side, so it looks spikey, before rubbing some Dax Wax in. I don't wear make-up. I'm not into any of that girly shit.

I pull on some skinny jeans, throw a hoodie over my uniform, do up my trainers, scoop up my pills, and go downstairs. Mum is sat at the breakfast bar; dressed in a thick fluffy navy-blue dressing gown, smoking. She's nursing a coffee and it isn't black. Which means it has Baileys in it. Mum looks at me, takes note of my face and looks down at the mug. I slam around the kitchen in protest, pouring some water to neck my pills, making a cup of coffee and a slice of marmite on toast. With every slammed drawer and cupboard door, Mum gets angrier.

"I know alright! I know! Stop fucking judging me!" She screams,

"Stop being so fucking pathetic then!" I yell at the back of her head, making her jump. I gulp down the coffee, shove the toast in my mouth, and slam the front door behind me as I leave.

∞

Our friends have arrived.

"How are you?" they all coo as coats are removed and they follow me into the kitchen, where I begin to prepare some drinks. The men grab ales and us ladies go for fizz with elderflower cordial, although my fizz is just fizzy water.

"How you are doing?" my friend asks me, checking my face for signs of my truth.

"I'm bearing up," I sigh, which is sort of true.

This is not my first rodeo after all, and in a way, I'm relieved I can't afford to pay for any more rounds of IVF after this one. I can't take what it's doing to me… To my body, or my mind. When I hyper stimulated, they told me that my ovaries had swollen up to the size of tennis balls and it would take months for them to go down again. I was not allowed to make any sudden movements in case I twisted up my fallopian tubes, which would have left me screaming in pain until they'd cut me open and untwisted them again. This meant I couldn't exercise. Plus... I went completely mad. Totally fucking batty. Like all my PMT's had come at once. Basically, I overdosed on oestrogen. Every month, since then, my PMT has made me loopy. Way worse and for way longer than anything I'd ever experienced before. What a joy! But I am just about better now. It has been six months and they've said I can go again. So here I am, injecting my belly once more, feeling like a human pin cushion. And I'm just about bearing up. Because I must. I've still got to try and hold down a job, keep my marriage together and put on a brave face for the world, even though my inner world, my spirit, and body are all in tatters.

∞

Sitting on the bench, looking out to sea, I think of Tom and the life we spent together. His drinking put a wedge between us that meant we were never able to fully be a normal couple. But we had muddled through as best we could, with me living separately in my safe, divine, cosy little flat in town, whilst he'd lived in his mystical gypsy wagon out in a field, where we spent our nights around the campfire signing, drinking and sometimes shouting. Looking out to sea, I remember our early days together, at the Roundhouse, and how utterly in awe I had been of the bastard. I'd been completely star struck by him back then. This incredible ballet dancer, over ten years my senior… I had fancied the tights off him.

But booze… It had stolen the man I loved from me. I could never be with him completely. It was like there was a cage between us; one he carried around with him everywhere he went. And with every drink the bars grew thicker. His soul became increasingly distant. It became ever harder to hear him, the real him, and to feel him; the man I loved. Until one day… He was gone. And this was a year or two before his actual death. I miss him so very much.

Patting the bench next to me, I realise I've been talking out loud to myself again. This makes me chuckle. I stroke the tulip along the back of the bench like a lover. Then lift the tulip to my lips and kiss its petals, tenderly laying the flower down on the seat.

"I'll see you next week Tom." I smile and pat the seat one more time for good luck, before rising and taking a deep breath of salty sea air.

A seagull hovers directly in my line of sight, over the cliff's edge, and for a moment, I can see the world through his eyes.

∞

The chambermaid entered and found Kitty sitting up in bed staring out of the window.

"Morning mistress" she curtsied and lay a tray of breakfast across Kitty's lap. It was a simple meal; bread, ale, eggs, butter, sugar, and currants. The butter had sage in it, at Kitty's request, as it was believed to help sharpen the wits.

Kitty could read. Her father had schooled her. He had schooled all his daughters. Partly because many of the cosmopolitan women at court could now read, but mainly, Kitty suspected, it was so he could talk at them, and for them to have some modicum of understanding as to what he was talking about.

His late wife had not understood a thing he had said, and she had thinly disguised her lack of interest in his diatribes. Kitty did not mind listening to him though, because she preferred his sermons on politics, news of the world and the prices of cloth, over listening to the prattle of the other women in the house. She had always felt closer to her father than anyone else, even though he always treated her with utter contempt. She cared not for him in a loving way. He was the kind of man one could not love. He was a foul tempered man who put social standing and ambition above all else, treating those he 'loved' like possessions to be bartered and traded with. And he was unpredictable, contrary, often changing his mind and behaviour based on his current society muse at court. And the thing he liked most in the whole wide world was the sound of his own voice.

He would lament continuously at having had no sons and being lumped with four daughters to pay for, but in truth Kitty did not think he could have been happy with sons either, as they would have no doubt stood up to him and his constant pontificating. And, as they grew older, they would have ended up doing whatever they wished to do, instead of having to follow his orders. Out of all the daughters, Kitty was the closest he'd ever had to the son he'd always wanted. Her independent and fiery spirit often got her into trouble, and in a strange way, this made her his favourite, even though he was awful to her.

But he was awful to everyone, unless he was flattering them. Although it had led him to sending her off to the village priest for correction.

∞

The bells chimed as Alice made her way through the village towards the church. The wild garlic was out, and she reminded herself to gather some on her way home to go with the bread and cheese that she had already prepared. Alice was dressed in her best linen dress, light onion brown in colour. It would be twenty summers old now, but she had kept it neat and only wore it on special days. It still looked pleasing, even though it no longer laced up tight, as her body had fattened a little with age. She tried to keep herself youthful looking. She had once been such a beauty and still was fair enough, but all the glamour of youth had left her now. John liked the way her dress brought out the colour of her big brown eyes. She made the dress for their pilgrimage to Winchester, her husband having brought her the material as a gift for their third wedding anniversary.

They had walked together for nine days, either sleeping on blankets beneath the stars, or in one of the churches along the way. And for one night they had even slept at an inn. That time they had spent together on the road - without any work to do, or folks to bother them about this and that, or with unwanted questions about their marriage bed; those days had been the happiest of her life. They had made love to each other beneath the stars every night, there and back again. Then at Winchester, they had been greeted by the Bishop himself, who had anointed and blessed them both before they had stepped nervously into the Cathedral. Alice had gasped at the sight of the place as she'd stepped foot inside, having never in her life seen anything so grand. She had fallen to her knees in reverence and prayed in thanks for the wonder of it all. All her concerns and troubles had seemed so small and petty in comparison to that majestic space. She had made her confession and mentioned her thoughts to the priest that mayhap her husband's late hours and heavy drinking had played a part in their difficulties. And the priest had chastised her and told her clearly that, for Eve had fallen and brought the first sin into the world, that barrenness cursing a marriage bed was from the wife's sinful tendencies and she should think of searching her own thoughts and wanton behaviour as to why God had not blessed them. She had been searching her soul ever since for the sins he had spoken of, but she was growing tired of looking.

She had prayed to God a dozen times a day, every day, for over twenty summers now, until it felt her soul would rip in two. She had also tried imploring the blessed Mary, whom she'd thought might have more sympathy, even though it were a cardinal sin these days to pray to her.

All she had to show for the pilgrimage and all the hours she had spent on her knees, both in prayer and in pleasing her husband, was this simple dress.

As Alice reached the gate to the church yard, following the stream of other villagers who were making their way up the path to the church door, she looked over at the great yew tree in the centre of the graveyard and her hand gently fell to her hanging pocket, still warmed by the cinnamon biscots and where the egg lay in wait, safely hidden within the cloth.

∞

Marjorie heard the church bells but was heading in the opposite direction. She had no intention of sitting and listening to that viper in the pulpit. He didn't even know the Ten Commandments or the Lord's Prayer by heart and had the audacity to call himself a priest. Obviously, she went to church from time to time, to keep everyone happy and so as not to be fined, but any chance she could find to not go, she took it. And today she had much more important things to do…

∞

My blood is boiling with fury. It's a twenty minute walk into town and to avoid the chaos for as long as possible, I choose a route that keeps me running along the top of the hill until I run out of land, and am forced to plunge down into Babylon. It's a sunny day, which means everyone is out and there is a jolly feeling in the air, so after ten minutes of stomping, I start to cheer up a little. I won't have to see my mum or brother for at least another twelve hours. I plan on going out and staying up until morning. I allow myself a few deep breaths of relief at the thought. Something sweet smelling catches my nose and the name 'honeysuckle' springs into my mind, even though I know nothing about plants.

The trees are covered in blossom and I suppose it could be them. Looking up at the bulging white blossoms against the blue sky I suddenly see how beautiful they are. Taking out my phone, I snap a shot. I have an app where I can design my own trainers using photos I've taken. The ones that work best are pictures of patterns. I smile at the image as I continue my walk to work; the blossom will look sick as a pair of trainers. I save the file and add it to the pile of other dream trainers I'll never have the money to buy.

∞

The four of us make our way through town and towards the festivities, which are taking place on the opposite hill. I used to live on this hill, back when I had first moved to the city, and it provokes so many memories of parties past it makes my head swing. Places I'd once got drunk, took drugs and screwed random guys… Plus the odd girl. Nearly every street on this hill has a sordid story attached to it, which makes me blush slightly now to recall. It feels like another lifetime. Six years of IVF has put pay to such shenanigans. These days I feel terribly middle aged and boring.

I've been working in a call centre now for two years, something I never thought would happen to me. Especially not at my age. I thought that by the time I was forty I would be a famous actress. When I'd lived on this hill, I'd been a drama student, filled with ambitions and dreams. But plan A hadn't worked out. Then plan B was having kids… And that's going pretty shit too. There is no plan C. Well, apart from… But no, I don't want to think about that today.

Today I am adorned in spring flowers, the sun is shining, and I am going to a sacred fertility festival that has been celebrated for hundreds, if not thousands, of years. Today I am opening my heart up to the possibility of the future; letting the spring magic work its way into my soul, into my heart, and into my womb. As we reach Queen's Park, at the very top of the hill, I feel like I have just completed a fertility pilgrimage and am reaching a sacred site. The field is full of beautiful people dressed in green gowns, with green painted skin, all covered in garlands of flowers. The trees are thick with blossom and everywhere there are stalls, hay bales and the sound of diddly diddly music. At the centre of it all, is a huge maypole.

∞

I make my way back towards town and head to the dentist. Here I am, sixty years old, and I still can't find a way to navigate the terror I'm feeling. I've even been to see a hypnotherapist about it, years ago now, and while I had been under the spell, or whatever they call it, I'd begun screaming. I was re-living some horrific memory. I asked Madam number one – Mum - if she knew of anything that had happened to me when I was younger that perhaps had caused me to feel such terror; something I had perhaps blocked out of my memory. My mother couldn't think of anything, but then my mother was not the best person to ask; she had always been a cold woman. Clearly on the spectrum, but the spectrum had not existed when she, or I, had been growing up. All we had known as kids was that our mother was a hard, stern, bitch. Devoid of any sympathy or empathy… And that she was mentally unwell.

She told me and my sister all our lives that we should never have children and how much she regretted having us. And we took that on board. Neither of us have had kids. I do not regret this decision in the slightest. As I walk through the streets of Brighton, the pavements are lined with bright young women whose faces are full of boredom and despair, while they plod along behind baby-laden prams. I have nicknamed Pavilion Gardens the *Land of Crushed Dreams.* I have never for one moment, felt like I've missed out. Not in the slightest. On the contrary, I feel like I dodged a bullet.

My mother would have been oblivious to any trauma suffered in my younger years and conceivably had been the one responsible for it. Which means that, although I can't pinpoint how the phobia started, it does not surprise me in the slightest that I have one.

I reach in my bag and take out a bottle of water and pack of ibuprofen. I pop two in my mouth and slosh them down. Then I step into the pub across the road from the clinic and order a tequila.

∞

Joan tugged hard at Kitty's laces, pulling the bodice tight against her ribs, making Kitty's back click. Kitty steadied herself by holding tight to the bed post. She stared out the window at the road below. Folks were making their way to the church and the bells had already begun to toll.

"Lift your arms Miss," commanded Joan as she slipped Kitty's fine silk dress down and over her corset, covering the bum-roll and petticoats. She pulled the material loose so that it tumbled to the ground and hung correctly. She turned Kitty about and pulled together the lacing at the front of the dress.

"We will be late" she muttered in annoyance, but Kitty had no desire to arrive at the church early. The priest would be in the pulpit already if they arrived late. Besides, everyone would be late this day. Kitty cared very little about such things. But Joan was cut from a different cloth and was growing increasingly frustrated at Kitty's disobedience. She set about brushing Kitty's hair, roughly, and tied it too tight around her head. It would bring on a headache, but Kitty intended to let it loose straight after the church service, so she did not complain. Brushing Kitty down with a clothes brush, like she was a horse, the maid told her to turn about and then quickly announced,

"There, you are done Miss, now be gone, or the service will have started."

"Thank thee, Joan" Kitty replied, and the maid curtsied and left the room curtly, taking the breakfast things with her. Kitty looked out the window and sighed at the sight of the other villagers bustling along merrily, intoxicated by the excitement of the feasting day.

"Peasants" muttered Kitty to herself bitterly. Then, cocking an ear and listening for Joan's footsteps descending the stairs, Kitty went to the fireplace and reached a hand up into the chimney. Pulling out a loose brick, she extracted a roll of paper. Returning the brick and wiping her hand on an old rag hidden beneath the wardrobe, she washed the last of the dirt from her hands in the wash basin. Unrolling the paper, she looked at it briefly before folding it into a rough square and wedging the parchment deep down in the recesses of her bodice. She smiled.

∞

The service was heavy, as Alice had expected it would be. It always was on feasting days. The priest seemed to feel the need to flex his authority over the parishioners on days when they were allowed a little taste of freedom and would perhaps partake in a touch too much ale. On days like this, the priest would lay on thicker than ever the dangers of succumbing to temptations. Indeed, some of the villagers were already well within their cups. Alice could smell the scent of ale hanging heavily in the air. And even without looking, she could guess who the guilty parties would be. Her husband being one of them. They were not stood together as they had arrived separately. She did not like to be at the church without him. It meant she must listen to the service as she did not have him to share a jape with or sideways glance. Not that there had been so many japes of late. These last few moons she had felt, though mayhap it had been her imagination, that he seemed to be more tired from work and less keen to spend time with her. In the pit of her stomach she fancied that he had changed towards her since she hit forty summers at Yuletide. As if it had been a milestone... Their hopes no longer able to be met. Though her courses were still strong and there were mistresses known of to bare babes at such an age... But not many. And often they died in the birthing. And for him, he could still go on to father many childer if given half the chance.

Alice reached out and grabbed the pillar in front of her, suddenly feeling light-headed. The fellow beside her took her arm and helped her stay on her feet. It was Peter, the blacksmith. She smiled and thanked him, reddened with embarrassment, and whispered that she forgot to break her fast. Peter smiled at her kindly, but also looked worried. All folks in the village were nervous about any signs of illness, ever since the sweating sickness reached Brighthelmstone. Alice pulled herself up-right and showed she could stand tall and unaided. She looked about the crowd for her good fellow, to see if he was anywhere near about, hoping she could shuffle over to him, but she could not see him anywhere. Her heart yearned for him desperately, but she told herself sternly that she would see him soon enough and tried, with all her might, to listen in earnest to the priest's sermon.

∞

As she reached the gate, Marjorie noticed that the garden needed tending. This was as she had suspected. The Master of the House, Nat was his name, was a goodly enough fellow, but he was over fond of the ale and did not see the level of work his good woman put in to keep their lives in order. Now that the babe had come, he was going to need to learn to pull his weight, or there would be no vegetables to eat, and Marjorie bet herself ten groats that the animals had not been cared for either. Mistress Abys was too kind a soul to scold him and they were most sweet upon each other, anyone could see that, but when a babe comes into the world, the father needs to learn to be a better man. That's just the way it is. Well, unless thou art one of the gentle folks... They have maids to be better men for them. That's why the rich are all so weak witted. *It be no good for thee,* mused

Marjorie, *being born of wealth. It tricks the mind into having false views of the world.*

This was another reason why she could not abide that priest. He was a strutting peacock. She liked the one before him, before he had passed on - bless his soul - he had been a humble man and had understood that some folks had been too long of the old faith and could not just throw out their previous beliefs. He had understood that if folks showed their respects and played by the rules of whatever the King had made up for them all to believe in that day, and if they kept their thoughts to themselves, it was best to just let them be. But this new priest, who had been 'new' for over ten summers now and would always be new as far as Marjorie was concerned, insisted that she played the part of the pious parishioner. And he lived like a Lord. The pompous pig. He would have her sent to the stake as a heretic if he ever glimpsed the truth in her soul and the feelings she kept hidden there.

Marjorie sighed. Any thought of the priest always wasted part of her precious day. She let it go and looked up at the beautiful sky and smiled. Taking a deep breath of hearty spring air, she knocked on the door to

Mistress Abys' cottage. It was unlocked, so she pushed it open and called within…

"Tis me Mistress Abys! Just thought I'd pass by to see how you and the babe are faring…" and she crossed the threshold to go within.

∞

Pushing open the door to the shop, I am blasted with the strong scent of coffee. I've managed to get here eight minutes early, so I've got just enough time for another cuppa before my shift starts. And I need it. My comedown is in full swing.

Matt's here already. He's gorgeous, gay and Asian. Oh yeah, and he adores me, much to the jealousy of everyone in the whole fucking world. I adore him too. We snogged once, back in the day, before he'd figured out he was gay, and I'd figured out I was gay too. I got him the job here. He's the only thing that makes being here bearable. Our manager, Spotty Vince, is a total tosser. A jobsworth, as my mum describes him. He takes obscene amounts of pleasure in getting all up in my personal and busting my balls over nothing. He thinks his little old 'manager' badge makes him the Queen of fucking Sheba. I hate him. If it weren't for

Matthew, I'd have quit long ago. Matt, who's making himself a coffee, indicates to me with ridiculous over-exaggerated hand signals that he'll make me one too, so I should grab a seat.

"I feel like a rat's crawled up my arse and died," he announces, smashing down two oat milk lattes and a couple of granola bars on the table, before flopping his gangly limbs onto the chair next me.

"You better not spend the whole shift farting" I warn him. "I'm serious. I'm gonna hurl if you fart today, Matthew. I swear!"

"Better not stand too near me then," he replies.

"Matt!" I snap, as I punch him, not particularly playfully, in his arm "I mean it! I feel like shit. I think I'm gonna hurl."

I drop my head into my arms dramatically and Matt realises that perhaps I'm not joking.

"Awww, are you feeling shit?" he changes tact and coos at me lovingly, as he rubs my shoulder.

"Yep..." I groan from between my arms. I look up and tell him, "and mum was already drinking when I got up this morning."

"Ah, shit," he replies throwing a coffee stirrer on the table in protest.

"And... Owen went out last night and got fucked up with a bunch of fucking rat kids and it looks like they burnt a load of stuff."

"What?" Matt asks, rearranging himself in the chair, genuinely shocked. He heard me roasting my brother last night, before lending him the tenner. "You're kidding?"

"He put a load of photos up on Facebook. He's such a knob..."

Matthew, who can sense when I'm about to embark on a rant, which will not be conducive to either of our moods, quickly interjects with a curve ball...

"Fancy a mushroom?" He asks, showing me the contents of his pocket.

"What? Oh..." The words that were about to spill out of my mouth pile up like a car crash on my tongue. "Where'd you get them from...?" We are always on the lookout for mushrooms.

"That guy I snogged last night had them. He said he can get us more. Do you want a little tickle? Help get us through the day?"

"I don't remember you snogging anyone" I reply. "And yes, I'd love one, now, please. Thank you… Hurry up…" No matter how awful I feel, mushrooms always make everything better.

He slips one dried Mexican mushroom to me under the table. I take it from him and pop it in my mouth. Giving it a good chew, I hope for the best.

∞

I place my hands on the maypole, having seen the *Wickerman* enough times to know the pole is an ancient symbol of fertility, and I need all the fertility vibes I can muster right now, so I push my belly against the wood and will its power to enter my womb.

Please work this time, I beg the universe, *Please, work…*

"He's a beaut' ain't he?" croons a cockney voice from right beside me.

I spin around in shock to see a man dressed from head to toe in a harlequin costume, smirking at me with a crooked trickster's smile. He licks his lips before speaking...

"Made of silver birch, he is," he says proudly, slapping the sides of the great trunk "The symbol of renewal and rebirth."

He looks over at me to check I'm interested, which I am, so he carries on...

"After a fire, or a forest has been cleared, it's the birch that first returns. Opportunist they are. Quickest draw in the Wild West, so to speak. It don't waste no time. Shoots when no one else is looking. Before anyone else has caught up. This here maypole is nearly thirty years old. He has borne witness to many a wedding and many a May Day, I can tell ya. He's stood us well... Is this your first time?"

My brain takes a moment to catch up with him, and when it does, I'm not sure what he means...

"First time, what?"

"At the May Day celebrations? Your first time here at our humble merriments?"

"Oh, I see! No, I've been here the last four, maybe... five years."

"Ah, I'd have thought I'd have recognised a beauty such as yourself, my lady. You should play the May Queen for us one day. We are always on the lookout for a fair maid in Brighton. There are not many who can call themselves maids in Brighton these days. And are you coming to see the play?"

"Well I'm not a maid," I respond, before quickly realising what I've just said and blush. To cover my embarrassment I ask, "erm, what play?"

The Harlequin grins a huge cheeky grin and begins to dance around me in a spritely fashion, calling loudly into the air in the most embarrassing manner…

"A play? A play you say… This day? A play? A fine play? Wouldst thou like to see a play? Well, you should take this from me my dear and come and see our fine players perform for your delight and merriment, upon this very eve. The finest performance you'll ever behold!"

He twirls and lands in a deep bow at my feet, then looks up at me, smirking with glinting eyes and murmurs under his breath "We'll still have you as a May Queen my dear. As I said… There's not many maids left about

Brighton these days, and you don't have to worry..." He raises himself up and comes close to my ear and whispers, "We don't check!"

He gives me a wink and hands me a flyer, then spins off into the crowd, jumping and clicking his heels twice in the air like a court jester of old.

I giggle loudly. *What a strange man!* I think.

Looking down at the slip of paper, I see that it reads;

Come one! Come all! And bring all yer chums! For this year's greatest show on earth! The tale of the Green Man... How he brings forth life with his very touch. And how he defeats the hand of the barren Holly King! Be warned... You might get pregnant just from watching it!"

I smile at the face of the leafy hand drawn fellow on the front of the flyer. It is clearly the harlequin guy. I fold the piece of paper and slip it in my pocket.

Well... I think, *I'll be having to go see that now won't I?*

∞

Sat in the dentist chair, I begin to panic. The dentist senses this and tries to ease my fears.

"I just need to have a look at first… I will only be using the mirror to move your mouth around so I can check the gums and behind your teeth. I promise I won't put anything else in your mouth without your permission. Is that okay?"

"I'm so sorry" I apologise, feeling awfully stupid for making such a fuss, but the dentist touches my arm gently. "It's not a problem, really, I promise. Now are you okay with me taking a quick look and I'll see if I can find out what's been causing you all this trouble?"

I nod meekly and lie back. Even just the act of opening my mouth to another person makes me feel sick with terror. When I close my eyes, my head suddenly begins to swim. I feel as if I'm being held down and my mouth is being pulled apart. I am seized with utter terror… I sit bolt upright and scream, right in the dentist's face. I'm mortified.

"I'm sorry, I'm so, so sorry…" I whimper in disbelief, wiping drool from my chin.

"Look, it's fine. Please don't apologise. Listen, I'm not meant to do this, but would you like some gas?"

She sees by my expression that this has taken me quite by surprise.

"I think it will help you to relax" she continues. "Just while I'm having a quick look. And it will also numb any pain if I touch the sore tooth by mistake. I can give you just a little, if you think it will help?"

"Yes please," I respond and begin to sob. My tooth is throbbing hard now, probably from the horror of it all, so I can't possibly leave here without getting it sorted. I feel such a wimp.

Taking a tissue from the dentist and wiping my eyes, I sit back and let the kind woman place a mask over my face. It is connected by a tube to a large canister, and as she begins to turn the release valve the mask hisses and fills with nitrous oxide. I take long slow breaths; once, twice…

My ears begin to buzz, and my vision turns to static. The buzzing in my ears deepens until it feels as if my whole body is shaking, every single molecule is vibrating and suddenly I can see space and light shining brightly between an eternal matrix of dots. Then I see they are all little fizzing atoms. I hear the dentist say to open my mouth, from somewhere that seems to be a long way off. I start to slip out of consciousness… The voice of the dentist disappears down a long dark tunnel. Everything is black. I'm in total darkness. Then I see a flash of light, as if a sack has been pulled off my head, and suddenly I'm surrounded by a circle of men, all standing over me. They come towards me, and I'm terrified. They engulf me; grabbing hold of my mouth, pulling it open wider and wider. It feels like they'll rip my skull in two. Then their encroaching shapes plunge me back into darkness. The light returns as a mottled, dappled movement, and I find I'm standing before a great, beautiful, yew tree, all twisting and turning with age. It's stunning against the deep blue sky and is covered in scraps of material and ribbons that flutter in the breeze. It goes dark again, this time as if someone just pulled a sack back over my head. Then I think I must have completely passed out, as all I remember is darkness.

∞

As Kitty approached the churchyard, there were one of two stragglers rushing ahead of her. Turning about and walking backwards, Kitty could see all the way back down to the green, where her father was hanging around by the barrels, talking and laughing with the other 'guards', but no one else was on their way to the service by the looks of things. She turned again and climbed the steep slope up to the churchyard. As she did so, the majestic ancient yew tree rose up into her view to greet her.

"Good day to thee," she whispered in reverence, with a warm smile, and as soon as she was close enough, reached out her lily-white hand and stroked the underside of one wide gnarly branch that hung heavy and low, covered in ribbons for May Day. As she passed by the giant split trunk, she whispered, "I will see thee later."

Then, at the heavy wooden door of the old flint church, she paused to take a deep breath. Collecting herself, she pushed it open. It squeaked loudly.

All turned and looked at her and she smiled brightly at the congregation, stepping briskly inside.

It was not worth being apologetic. Kitty discovered long ago that she would be punished whatever she did, so she might as well not grovel. Best let it all wash over her like the way water runs from a duck's back. This realisation, which had come to her mayhap two or three summers past, made her fearless. Now she did whatever she wished. Last night, she stole out of the house in her father's riding clothes, so no one would know that she was a maid out on the road alone, and had climbed all the way to the top of Windover Hill, where she played amongst the ruins of the ancient fort that crowned the downs above the Long Man's head. She had sat and watched the crescent moon dancing playfully across the waves of the sea, out on the distant horizon, along with the glistening little lights of Brighthelmstone. She had spun in circles bare foot beneath the stars, until she'd fallen to the floor; dizzy with delight. Even now the memory of it all brought such a delicious wave of elation at the freedom of it all. Kitty hated being born a maid and wished with all her heart that she might somehow be a man. God could do anything, if he willed it to be so. It was what she prayed for in every prayer and had done so for as far back as she could remember.

∞

Alice turned and saw the young girl enter the church; all snooty in her fancy frock and with the air of one who may do whatever she pleased. Alice did not know her well, but she knew her father and he was a total arse. Always complaining at the work both the dairy and the bake house did, as if he could do any better himself, with his soft maid's hands that had never seen a day of work in their lives.

The sermon was now in full swing and Alice felt that every moment was lasting an eternity. She could not breathe and her legs ached from standing. She looked about the church again to see if she could find John and caught sight of him at the far end, almost hidden by a pillar. Her heart leapt with joy. He was laughing and she smiled to see his big beautiful bearded face and wondered what the jest had been. She had not been listening to the priest, so did not know what John would be mocking in his head, but she smiled along with him anyway, in the hope that he would see her and think she knew his mind. But then she saw a small coifed head bob forward from the pillar, also laughing, and to her horror it was Marigold, the brewer's daughter.

Marigold had mayhap nineteen summers or so and glowed repressively with youth. But it was not just her youth that glowed; she had grown into such a beauty. With green eyes and curling brown locks of hair, and a fine pair of round full duckies that forever spilled wantonly from her bodice.

All the men in the village fawned upon her and had done so since she was a child. But she was a child no more. Her nearness to great quantities of ale only aided her appeal. Alice might have been a dairy maid, and everyone loved a dairy maid, as their hands were soft and their skin lily white, but everyone sure as hell loved a brewer's daughter even more. Her dress smelt of hops for Christ's sake! Not old milk.

Alice's heart leapt into her throat and she promised herself that her plans for this eve must be followed through with, for she was close to losing her fellow. It was plain to see that his eyes were wandering, and she was losing his heart.

DAMN YOU! She screamed in her head to the heavens.

∞

Marjorie found Mistress Abys sat in a high-backed, comfortable chair by the fire, with the babe at her breast. She was well enough. She told Marjorie they had named their daughter Bess, after the princess, because she had red hair; a feature inherited from her father. Thinking on the father, Marjorie noticed that the fire was nearly out.

"Where is your good fellow?" asked Marjorie, as she lowered herself down, with a lot of huffing and puffing, to tend to the embers; blowing long and slow breaths onto the glowing charcoal to catch the kindling she'd placed expertly about. A flame flared up and Marjorie set about building a stack of larger logs, surrounding the licking flames.

"He'll be at the green Mistress, helping the other fellows to guard the maypole."

And quaff the ale, thought Marjorie, as she slapped her hand on her knees and rose herself up again; using all her strength to fight against the forces of the earth.

"So, he'll be at the festival this day, will he?"

"Aye, but he said he will call on me after the service and bring me back some hog flesh."

Marjorie sighed.

"Don't go spoiling him and leave him thinking you can manage to do this all on your own. You can't. How are you to tend the fire, go to the jakes, or eat your victuals, with a child hanging at your breast? You have no cot to put her in safely. You don't want her rolling off the board or the rats to get her on the floor…"

"I know, Mistress Marjorie," agreed Abys, "but he is doing his best. I swear he is! And he left me plenty of cheese and bread on the board, so I can eat if I get hungry."

Marjorie looked over at the board and saw some dirty looking plates of stale bread and cheese, crawling with flies. Tutting to herself, she went over and flapped the flies away, covering the cheese with some cloth.

∞

The mushrooms have kicked in and are very much taking the edge off the day… The shift and my life. I feel like I'm being carried around on a cloud. My stomach still isn't happy, but the pain in my head has gone.

And I don't want to kill everything and everyone. I'm having quite a pleasant time in fact. I find that with mushrooms, they make me feel like my heart is open. I feel kind of in love and connected to everyone. And people seem to open their hearts to me more in return. Me and Matthew take mushrooms whenever we can get hold of them, but we try to keep some back for work, to save us from what is otherwise hell on earth. Matthew is being fucking hilarious today and I suspect he's taken quite a few more than me. He keeps losing his shit, giggling like a kid at everything, and getting confused about what it is he's doing, then laughing at himself for that too, all whilst trying to work the coffee machines. It certainly makes the shift go by quicker.

A jingle jangle sound comes through the door, and I look up to see a jester walking in. A fucking jester. This isn't the mushrooms, there really is a fucking jester in the café. Matt is on the floor with laughter and I have to get him to his feet and usher him into the back room, trying to pull myself together before I go back in to serve.

The guy is covered in a red and green diamond patterned Lycra outfit and he's carrying a staff covered in bells. I smile as brightly as I can, absolutely loving the absurdity of life (I literally live for this shit), and greet him with a…

"Good afternoon sir, what can I get for you?"

"Good afternoon sir. I don't know… What CAN you get for me?"

I turn red, wondering if it is obvious that I'm on mushrooms, whilst also loving the fact he just called me sir. I REALLY like the way that sounds… "Sir!" Oh yes, that is good. Better than lady. I hate being called a lady.

The man has such a cheeky smile and he is looking right at me, as if he's peering into my soul.

"Soooo," he replies with a wry smile. "Can you get hold of anything interesting?"

∞

The day draws on and my friends are starting to get a bit intoxicated, as is my husband. I don't begrudge them, but it is becoming rather dull being the only sober one. And it's making me feel tired and disconnected. I keep thinking about the flyer in my pocket. I do fancy going to see the play, but I can tell that the others will not be in the mood for it now, so I think perhaps I'll go without them. The thought of this is partly terrifying and partly thrilling. The music starts around the maypole. Someone is playing a shabby looking set of bagpipes, made from what looks like an old animal skin, and they are joined by a majestic smiling giant who plays the fiddle like an old ancient bard. The beautiful girls, dressed in green and adorned with garlands, skip merrily about the crowd, grabbing folks to join them. One goes to grab my husband's hand, but he shakes his head, saying;

"She'll do it!" and pushes me forward.

"Go on then," I laugh, and she grabs me and leads me to the pole. She hands me a red ribbon and says breathlessly, "This symbolises your menarche, your first bleed; the moment when you first became a woman."

I turn red with embarrassment. Why do I not know this? I'm not prudish, but this is the first time I've ever heard the word 'menarche' and it instantly transports me back to the first time I bled…

I had been at a guy's house with these two boys, all on my own, which was terribly exciting as I adored them both and suddenly had them all to myself. I fancied one of them like crazy and the other one I had used to go out with. The pair were basically the centre of my world at the time and it was very rare that I got to be on my own with them. I was relishing every second of it. The guy whose house it was made us coffee, something that also never really happened at that point in my life, and I heard the one that I liked, tell the awful gag: "I like my coffee, like I like my women, black and sweet." I didn't realise at the time it was a well-known joke and thought he really meant he only liked black women. He was really into hip hop. Tribe Called Quest were playing on the HiFi and the guys kept leaping up and reciting the lyrics whilst trying to bust out rap moves. The one guy, the guy I liked, was being annoying. I knew I had power over him. We were all friends from the local drama club, and we had performed together in Cinderella over Christmas. I had played Cinderella and my ex had been Buttons. The one I liked now had been part of a comedy duo who came on and did funny turns here and there throughout the play. He would often go on just before one of my Cinderella scenes. We would wait together in the darkness of the wings and I would come up close behind him and whisper in is ear and stroke his neck, just before he went on the stage. It was one of the most erotic moments of my life. I could feel how much I was turning him on and how he was putty in my hands. But at that moment later in the house, in front of his mate, he was acting like he didn't even know I existed. Eventually I left, feeling annoyed and frustrated. I couldn't be bothered with their nonsense.

When I got home, I found out I was bleeding. It's funny, as I always think of my first bleed when I hear Tribe Called Quest, playing, but I hadn't thought about that being the moment I became a woman or known that there was a name for my first bleed... Menarche.

I look up at the towering pole rising-up into the bright blue sky and suddenly clock what the while ribbon represents.

Then we are dancing. Spinning in circles, under and over, under and over, weaving the ribbons in and out, spiralling onwards and forwards, around and around, weaving though time and space.

∞

I leave the dentist in somewhat of a daze. After the gas, it has been most strange. The dentist told me I needed to come back for a root canal and I didn't even bat an eyelid; I was too floaty to care. In the bright and beautiful afternoon sun, I now find that I'm facing up at the fluttering leaves of a large Plane tree, letting the dappled light play over my face. It is making patterns dance behind my closed eye lids. Back at the surgery, in my gas-induced state, I'd picked up a flyer as I left the reception. The image had caught my eye; it was of a Green Man. I open my eyes and look at the image, squinting in the bright light and turn it over. It's for a play that's on tonight in a venue near Wilmington, out past Lewes way. It's being performed by the group who put on the May Day thing up in Queen's Park each year. Hmmm, I'm in the mood for a spot of May Day festivities, seeing as it's such a gorgeous day and I'm feeling all floaty...

I look back at the tree, and for a moment, I remember the fluttering ribbons on the yew tree in my vision. They'd danced languidly on the wind. Focusing again on the tree before me now, I see the character of a younger, more elegant specimen, with its expressionist mottled bark. Then I see the Green man peering back at me, within the twists of the trunk, in all his leafy splendour. I smile and whisper.

"Hello friend!"

I do not believe in coincidences. Kairos is my champion and I know all things happen at the correct and perfect time. This moment feels like I'm bathing in Kairos.

"I'll see you later then," I smile up at the tree, placing the flyer safely back in my pocket and I begin to make my way across town to my god daughter's house.

∞

Kitty pushed her way through the crowd and into the church. There was a seat for her at the front of the congregation. Her blasted father paid for all the family to have seats installed at the front, but he was not there, and she did not want to look at the priest, so she strategically placed herself behind a pillar. It was bad enough that she must listen to him. The room smelt even more rancid than normal, as the fellows had been at the ale and clouds of farts hung strongly in the air. Kitty reached around and pulled up the pomander that hung from her belt. She did not care if the villagers thought she was rude. She thought it was rude of them to stink the place out. Kitty sighed. In very truth, she would have been most pleased if any of the villagers ever looked at her with even a spot of kindness in their eyes or spoke to her with any pleasantness in their words. Joan was the closest thing she had to a friend, yet her maid did not like Kitty and would not keep her secrets. Kitty, to her, was no more than a job.

It was her all father's fault.

He had grown rich from selling cloth in London after taking his mother's weaving there when he had had only seventeen summers. The sheep on the downs made particularly fine wool, and he thought the cloth his mother wove would fetch a good price in the city. His gamble paid off and soon he was clothing the gentle folk at the King Henry's court. Having made his fortune, he became himself welcomed within the court as one of the new breeds of celebrated merchants. And he never let anybody forget about it, keeping his daughters in the finest of gowns, almost like they were walking market stalls, presenting his wares.

Kitty wished she was not so set apart from the other girls in the village, though she was glad she was not stupid. She found it almost impossible to converse with some of the villagers she met. She had more understanding of her horse then the wit of some of the common folk.

But she was so desperately lonely. And her father grew ever more distant, as his work increasingly took him to the Low Countries. He was often away at sea for months at a time. And soon he would have her married off and… Oh, she could not bear to think upon that and pinched herself hard so she would not cry. Not here. Not in front of these folk.

∞

Alice had preferred the sermons when they were in Latin. It had been more like a performance, along with the actual Mystery Plays that had brought all the local parishes together, creating such splendid spectacles.

She missed those most of all, and the incense and the chanting. Now it was just this fellow harking on at them in the common tongue for hours upon hours on end. There was not even a stain glass window to look upon; them all having been smashed and replaced with plain glass. There were just a couple left to the sides of the church, but it was thought papist to stand and stare at them, instead of straight ahead at the priest. She really missed the pretty stained glass windows. And they had taken such a long time and a great deal of skill to make. The glass blowers must have been mortified to see them smashed to pieces…

She often thought that mayhap God was punishing her for following this new faith. Mayhap this was the sin that the priest had meant? But she refused go to the stake for a God who would not willingly give her a child in the first place. It was a spiteful circle she went through around and around in her head. He was punishing her for the new faith, but he had already not given her a child already. She had been thirty summers when the country had broken from Europe and named itself its own sacred state.

Folks had been mixed about it all. In many ways, a change had been coming. All knew the priests were up to crooked things, with secret ways of making money and hurting those who stopped them. It was quite terrifying what they had been able to do. But to break from his holy father the Pope and Europe? None of them really thought that this would be possible. Let alone that the whole faith would be turned inside out. And then here they were, with priests just as bad as the ones they had had before, if not worse. Just a whole new lot, with a great less grandeur. At least the old faith knew how to put on a good show. Many folks had stopped coming to Sunday mass, so many in truth that the bailiffs had levied a fine on the heads of anyone who did not attend without good reason. Which did not win any favours. It had almost become a fast. But not a very funny one.

Alice felt she would suffocate if she did not leave soon. Her hand reached instinctively to the egg in her pocket and she looked over at her fellow. He stood close to Marigold; he would be able to smell her from there and mayhap some parts of their bodies were touching. Some accidental pressing up of limbs against each other. Or worse; they were not moving and looked as if they were listening intently, which was always a sign that a pair of folks were up to something suspicious.

∞

Marjorie brewed Mistress Abys a hot posset of brewer's yeast, raspberry leaf, fennel, stinging nettles and milk thistle, to aid with her milk flow. She then cleaned up the humble dwelling. She took the babe whilst Abys visited the jakes and gave herself a quick wash down. Marjorie suspected she had not washed since the birth, for without the aid of her husband, how would she have been able to? She wondered if he had even held the babe yet. When Abys returned, all freshened up and tucking her hair back up into her coif, Marjorie showed the young mistress how to swaddle her baby so she could leave her daughter safely on the board whilst she went to the jakes or had anything else she needed to do. And Marjorie decided in her mind to ask about the village to see if any mothers had an old cot they no longer had use of. Her fellow could have cobbled one together by now… but had he hell. She would have stern words with him when she saw him later.

The bells began to toll, marking the end of mass, which meant it was time for Marjorie to make her way down to the green for the festivities, checking in on Mistress Anne on the way. As Abys sipped on the posset, Marjorie gave the fire another stoking and a few more logs, then saw that Abys ate some cheese and bread, before leaving the darkness of the cottage and returning to the bright light of the dazzling noon sun. She took a deep breath, smiling at a job well done, and made her way down the lane towards the sound of the merriment and music beginning to drift up from the green.

∞

The sermon came to an end and there was an audible sigh of relief from the congregation, as the bells begun to toll joyfully, and the villagers started to pour out of the church. Kitty let herself be dragged out of the church door, enjoying the close contact with other human bodies, but then she pulled herself up against the yew tree, as everyone else bustled past, letting the main flow of folks pass by. The warmth of the sun hit her face in a shimmering dance through the needles of the tree and the air was still fresh and full, with the smell of spring.

The lambs in the field next to the church bleated in excitement at the sight of so many people suddenly appearing; their little calls peppering the gossip and chatter of the parishioners. Kitty took a deep breath and smiled. On a day such as this, it was impossible to be unhappy. Then she heard the voice of the priest, making his way outside, so she turned and threw herself back into the crowd, allowing herself to be carried away with the tide. As they hit the street, she looked around at the hill above the Longman, where she had danced bare foot and free the night before, checking to see if there were any signs of her guilt reflected back at her from the grassy banks, but all she could see was an empty lane, but for a waddling fat crow and bobbing wagtail. The Longman peered back at her knowingly though, through his fairy gateway.

As she turned back, she saw a mistress looking at her strangely. One of the ostlers, who tended to the horses. A blonde-haired woman, who always seemed to be at the centre of unpleasantness about the village.

She was known as Mary or May or some such name. She was a bitter woman and Kitty did not like her, but she liked even less how the woman was looking upon her now, so she gathered up her skirts and walked past briskly, shooting her a quick "good day" as she went.

VIRGIN

"You are braver than I had imagined you would be. I'm proud of you. You didn't grow up.

Reality is magical isn't it? The greatest spell on earth...

I like what you did with my creativity… Stoked it like a fire, trained it like a wild horse and showed up every day, overcoming so many obstacles and perceived failures. And you're still doing it; even after all these years. Even though you never 'made it' in any real sense. I doth my coif to you mistress, you've kept it real. I think that THIS is your greatest achievement.

Overall, we've got through this pretty much unscathed, haven't we? I mean, shit has happened, but you didn't decide to let the things that went wrong impede your growth. You still look pretty much the same as you did as a sapling. There's a couple of kinks in the old trunk, but we all love a little bit of kink now don't we.

I've loved all the sex we've had… Well… Except for the #MeToo's of course but, see above… We *didn't let them destroy us or the enjoyment we have of our body. I like that you've finally fallen back in love with your body again. You've taken good care of it… And hun, you're 40 and hardly anything is wrong with it, so… *high five*! Long may that last. And I don't care if you get a bit fat now. The glamour of youth is fading, and it's being replaced by something more gentle, strong and substantial. It doesn't require you to be thin. Eat that cheesecake for me. It looks yum.*

I feel like we have nailed each phase of life thus far. Which is a thing I know you feel uncomfortable about saying in public, because it sounds so big headed, but I don't care, I'm fifteen, I don't give a shit! We have done. We had a great time at school, we had a great time in our teens, and we had a great time in our twenties. The early thirties were pretty shit, but they also taught us not to be cocky and showed you how to accept defeat gracefully. You would have made a good mum, but I never wanted kids anyway, so personally I'm not that fussed. Sorry… I know it has been hard for you and is still your greatest sadness.

Cor, hormones are bastards, aren't they?

I've got a theory… I reckon that adolescence isn't really all about the hormones… I think that the most difficult part of being a teenager is realising that adults are all lying to you. All that good and evil shit you're taught as kids. One day you wake up and realise that all the adults you've ever known are doing evil shit all the time. Then you discover you must also force your own sweet self into a deformed shape that the world requires of you. And to do this you have to get evil too. What a sticky, ugly, neon, crass, gilded shaped 'world' it is. What the actual fuck is that all about?

Let's get serious for a second though... That's not really the world is it? No, the real world is weeds growing up through the cracks in the pavement and the fields beyond the cities. You're all gonna die soon, you know that don't you? How you've been treating the planet... It's going to kill you. And no one is doing anything about it. I mean, how can people not care about this shit? I mean, I know you "care", but I'm talking about caring enough to do something about it. Governments need toppling. Seriously, it's the ONLY THING THAT MATTERS!!! How can anyone sleep at night knowing that 50% of the wildlife on this planet has gone in the last 25 years? Since I got popped out and you became a woman, or whatever the archetype is between virgin and mother... Sacred whore? I don't know... Since then... 50% of Mother Nature's bounty has gone up in a puff of smoke. Literally smoke. The bible says that God gave Adam and Eve one job and that was to take care of the plants and the animals. Fucked that one up, didn't you? One job… And you've totally screwed it. And then you wonder why teenagers are killing themselves and each other, wracked with misery and depression?

I want to scream and scream and scream and scream and scream. But instead, I wrote a teenage angsty poem, because that's how I deal with things…

Wear Sunscreen

As I sit on this plastic garden chair,
That'll take centuries to decompose,
Absorbing the sunshine into my pores,
The fear in my body grows...
Because it is October
And it's really really hot.
The temperatures are rising,
And no one gives a jot.
Weather systems are revolting,
With storms beyond compare.
The ice caps are all melting,
And no one seems to care.
Game of Thrones is happening,
Beneath my very nose.
Distractions of in fighting,
Over a worthless iron throne.
When all the while beyond the wall,
Of a media smokescreen,
The real problems mobilise,

And they will wipe us clean.
The temperatures are rising,
And we'll all need a drink...
But our water tables are being bought,
By scum bags, who will sink
So low as to screw us all
For every single drop,
And we'll be too busy fighting
For anyone to stop
The truth that is unfolding
Before our very eyes;
That the rich are buying our water,
As they poison our very skies.
And our neighbours across the road from us
Are not our mortal foe.
It's the fuckers who own the papers,
And the factories, and the dough.
They're scooping up our resources,
Whilst contaminating the rest.
And building giant bunkers,
Luxurious safety nests.
Because they know what is coming,
And it's not gonna be fun...
So you'd better have an underground spring,
And you'd better have a gun.
But the short sightedness is harrowing,
Because no matter how well they dwell
In their shitty little bunkers,
We're all going to hell.
These changes are irreversible,
And there'll be no turning back.
You can't put water in a bucket,

When the bucket has a crack.
We're screwing up the planet,
And we haven't another one...
So enjoy your futile fucking fights,
And enjoy the extra sun.
Soon you'll be wishing for winter,
And lawns of lushes green,
And butterflies and bees and birds,
And fishes in the sea.
All that will be left of us is floating now in space,
The Satellite Voyager,
Representing the human race.
55 different greetings,
From brothers and sisters across the world,
Showing a united front,
On a disc of brilliant gold.
But the truth is we're divided,
And it will be our demise,
As we listen to the telly,
And suck in its triad of lies.
It's all that will be left of us,
As our planet dies forever...
Summer is coming,
And the days will be long and full of terrors.

Anyhoo… Why is the way adults behave so insane? I literally don't understand how you can live with all this bullshit. But I guess not everyone is… People keep killing themselves, don't they?

Don't you go killing yourself now please. I want you to live. I want you to fight. I want you to make a difference. And I want to see what happens. How it all turns out. I know this means that sometimes you will go through a rough ride, on my behalf, but the bad times won't last forever. That's one of the main things we've learnt together, hey.

I love you… I've not forgotten you. I'm always here. And now you are all the things I ever wanted to be… Grown up, living your own life, doing whatever you want, whenever you want. It's all I dreamt of. I'd give my right arm to be where you are now. Would you give your right arm to be where I am again? If you would then… Swapsies? I'll happily take your place and show you how it ought to be done.

Seriously though. I love you. You're going to be okay. Keep on trucking. You're doing good… You've got this."

DUSK

The setting sun's golden rays hit one of the last remaining stained glass windows and bathed the three women locked up inside in such furious light, it was as if they were all on fire. They had not yet spoken to each other. They were still full of shock and disbelief at what had just happened. Alice could not stop wringing her hands, nor taking her eyes from the door, willing her good man to come to her aid, to stop this foolishness and take her home. Her heart was beating so fast in her chest, she felt she might be sick. For some time, she had forgotten to breathe.

They were all silent as mice before a cat. Alice glanced over at Will's daughter; the one who had been late to church this morn. She was sitting staring up at the plain window above the altar, which was blazing with golden light, framing the boughs of the large old yew tree outside. The cunning woman, Marjorie, sat on the other end of the bench to Alice, spinning with a drop spindle, as if she had not a care in the world.

Alice's leg was thumping with pain. One of the fellows, Nat was his name, the husband of Mistress Abys who worked with Lettys at the potters, kicked her hard in the back of her calf as she struggled to explain herself to the men who had set upon them suddenly in the graveyard. Now she could not put her foot down flat on the floor and it hurt terribly. She felt she knew Nat a little and was sure he had always been a friend of John's. She was also sure that when John found out what Nat had done to her; he would kill him for it. She did not know Mistress Abys well, but she had always been friendly enough to her and given her a friend's-sized portion of cheese and fat whenever she'd come and visited the dairy. Well, Alice would be damned if she'd ever be giving Mistress Abys a friend's-sized portion again. Though she did not wish to think on being damned right now…

As soon as John heard tell of what had just happened, he would be here in no time, smashing in the heads of whoever stood guard outside. And he would give that Nat his guts for garters.

Nat had been so furious. Alice had never seen a fellow so wracked with wrath before in all her summers upon the earth. His face had been bright red and looked as if it might pop off his neck. He would not listen to them… the women. They had shouted and shouted at him, but it was as if they were not there. Instead, he just yelled to the other men that "These women are all in league with the devil". And the cunning woman had been shouting back at him, with a mouth so foul, Alice had never heard such things from a woman's mouth before, cursing him with words she had only ever heard inside an alehouse. She had screamed in Nat's face that he was idle and had not tended to his wife…

Fancy him calling it a heathen's feasting day! He had got that from the priest's sermon this morn… But he'd never had any qualms before at quaffing great quantities of ale at the 'heathen' days of springtime's passed. Alice could not recall ever seeing the fellow without a vessel pressed to his lips.

Alice looked back to the wooden door and willed it to open with all her heart, and for her good husband John to be there on the other side, arms outstretched, with tears in his eyes at the thought of losing her... His dearest one... His good wife...

∞

The church was growing darker and Marjorie was finding the spinning increasingly difficult to see. Mistress Alice, the dairy maid who had come to her at Imbolc, was sat beside her, on the other side of the bench, nearest to the door. There was a young maid in there too with them, who had got bundled up into the church. It had surprised Marjorie to discover she'd been hiding up the tree. Now the girl was perched on a cushion by the altar. Marjorie recalled she had birthed her, her being the merchant's daughter.

She knew not why they were all in there, but that Master Nat had been at the root of it to be sure. He had been shouting and spitting, saying something about Mistress Anne being dead and how Marjorie had poisoned his wife and turned her against him. He had spat at her, right in her face, and called her a wretched old beggar woman. She had shouted back and let him know, in no uncertain terms, that if Mistress Abys was sick then it was for the rancid victuals he had left for her to eat, and that he was an idle bastard who'd been too much at the ale. That was when Mistress Alice had tried to speak to him, and he had stamped hard on the back of her leg. They had all heard something pop, like a cork from a bottle. That was when they had become compliant and did as they were told, letting the men lock them up in the church. Marjorie could see that Alice's leg was not broken... It had not been the bone that had popped, but the sinews beneath the skin. There was nought she could do for the woman whilst they were locked up in here. If they had been outside, then she would have made up a poultice from yarrow, to reduce the swelling and aid the healing, but she would not find any yarrow growing in amongst these stone walls. It would take many weeks of rest for the injury to heal, but that was by far the least of the woman's troubles.

Marjorie tried to sneak a glance at the two women, to gain a measure of where they might be at in their wits and humours. In her reckoning, they would be in here now for the night, whilst someone from the village rode to Brighthelmstone and returned with the magistrate in the morn. That was what happened with Mary Childcraft. They locked her up in the church overnight, then in the morning the magistrate had arrived, interrogated her for two days without letting her sleep, got a confession out of her for being a witch - a servant of the devil - then they'd hung her the same day as the trial. Marjorie had overheard from some drunk fellows set to wild boastations, staggering home in the darkness one night, that some fellow, or fellows possibly, had gone and had their wicked way with Mary, despite her age, as part of the interrogation, or mayhap after she had confessed. Marjorie knew no more details than this. But she did know, that it had happened because they'd known they'd get away with it. No one would have helped her or believed her once she had been accused. Marjorie knew not who it was or if it were for certain true, but if it was, they had made sure Mary could not tell anyone of what they had done. The day they had hung Mary her mouth had been toothless and bloody.

Marjorie flicked a glance over at the young one. If she remembered rightly, her name was Kitty. She had delivered her; Marjorie remembered it clearly now. Her mother had died soon after as she would not stop bleeding. Marjorie eyed the young wench across the golden light. She was a fair maid. They'd all be wanting to have their wicked way with that one... Not only for her looks, but also to teach her a lesson for always being so high and mighty with such airs and graces. Mind you... If they would have their way with Mary Childcraft, then they would be all over the dairy maid Alice too. She was plump and youthful looking still, despite her age. Everyone liked a dairymaid after all. What a boon that would be for them. They would think it be the start of feasting day all over again. She was surprised they had not set upon them already, what with the whole village being well within their cups. But she supposed Kitty's father was the reason for that. No one would wish to be caught messing about with his daughter, not until she had been rightfully condemned. Then it would all be fair game, for she would be going to the gallows anyway. Marjorie had thought her father would have come fetch her by now and wondered why he had not? She did not think John would come for Alice. The gossip was that John the Baker had been at it with the Brewer's daughter for some time now, so he would be well shot of Alice.

Poor love. But the young one… Now she was a dark horse who had kept herself to herself. In truth, Marjorie knew no reason why her father would condemn her like this. But condemned her he clearly had…

∞

Kitty was sat on a cushion on the floor, up at the altar. An observer might have thought she was at prayer, and the other two women probably thought she was, but her eyes were looking above the altar to the window where the yew tree boughs danced gently in the last of the Beltane light. Her thoughts were on her father. As soon as he heard news of what had befallen in the churchyard, he would be here post-haste, to free her from these confines. Really, it was such a jest that any of those fellows would dare lay a finger upon her, them all knowing who her father was. And that look in their eyes. It was as if they had been happy to see her. She had seen that look before and knew what it meant.

That woman had been with the men; the Ostler who had looked at her strangely after church. Perhaps she had seen her out dancing under the stars last night? She had gone to the stables to steal her father's riding clothes... Perhaps she had spied on her there?

Kitty peered longingly at the window, willing her father to arrive; hoping for this nonsense to soon be over, so she could go home and get into her large warm bed. Tell her mother in her prayers all about the folly that had just taken place.

"Tis him!" the plump woman yelped, as she leapt from the bench, in what seemed like one jump, across the floor to the door; listening intently to whatever noise she thought she had heard outside. Kitty had heard nothing, but the woman's sudden action had made her jump out of her skin.

For a long time, there was silence. The woman leaning desperately towards the door. Then the old one went back to spinning and Kitty returned her attention to the window.

After a long pause the plump woman admitted defeat, and with an exasperated sigh whispered to herself "Where art thee?"

"Who?" asked Kitty, this time making the Mistress jump.

"My husband..." replied the woman curtly. Then to herself she whispered, "My good fellow."

"Doth thou expect him to come?" smirked the older woman, who was spinning at the other end of the bench and Kitty saw now that these two women knew each other. Kitty did not know the plump one. She looked the same as all the other peasants in the village. Perhaps she had seen her before, but she had no way of knowing. She did, however, know the older one. She was the local wise woman. People called her a witch. She thought that perhaps her parents had known her as her father had mentioned her in passing.

"He will come!" snapped the plump one "He doth love me."

"What of thy childer?" Kitty asked, hoping that mayhap the woman had a brace of strapping sons, who might be on their way, flocking to her aid. "Will they not come for thee?" but the woman glared at her across the cold stone emptiness.

Kitty got the feeling this woman did not like her. And she knew not why. They had only just met. Well... Kitty was used to people not liking her and she cared not... She returned to the window. Her father would be here shortly anyway and then this nonsense would be of no consequence…

∞

Alice returned to her seat. Her leg hurt terribly and gave way beneath her as she stepped upon it. Faltering and grabbing hard at the wooden bench, she managed to lower herself inelegantly back down onto the seat. She saw that Marjorie had noticed, but at least the old woman had the decency to look away and Alice returned to staring at the door… *John will be here shortly,* she thought. *Any moment now…*

"Be that what thou wert doing by yonder tree?" Marjorie asked suddenly, and it took Alice a moment to realise she was talking to her, and then another moment again to understand what she'd meant by it. She thought to herself that *yes, it was what she had been doing by yonder yew tree, but it be none of that old hag's business, thank thee very much. And the reason why they were all in this mess was because SHE had been here. Caught alone with the cunning woman, at twilight on Beltane...* Then Alice caught her breath as she suddenly reflected on what this looked like… How it would be read by the other villagers. If she had heard of another Mistress from the village being caught at the yew tree with the cunning woman... Well, she would think it sounded wicked for sure. She would think…

"Doth thou not think, it seemed as if they were waiting for us?" Alice blurted out suddenly and with more venom than she had intended. Instantly regretting being so vile, she tried to pull herself together and went back to looking at the door.

"Where art my husband?" she implored.

"Where art my father?" responded the young maid meekly.

"And where art my jackdaw?" asked Marjorie.

The two women shot her a glance.

Time slipped by.

Alice stared hard at the door, willing it to open. She began to think on how she had been passing through that door all her life. She had been baptised in here, and had taken her holy communion here, when they had all still followed the old faith. Then she had been married to John here.

Tears pricked her eyes suddenly when she thought on this and she had to work hard to push them back. There was no reason for her to cry. John would be here shortly. Then she thought of Marigold, and how John had looked at her with hungry eyes, in this very place earlier in the day, and the tears sprang back up again. She shook her head and turned her mind from such thoughts, instead dreaming on what she would do when John did come to fetch her. That was when she remembered her hanging pocket and how it still contained the egg and bisocts. The men had been too busy bustling her and the two other women into the church to search them properly, though they had taken their knives. Marjorie had even manged to keep hold of her basket somehow, which is why she was now able to sit here infuriatingly drop spinning. The stupid old crone. If she had not been at the tree...

∞

Marjorie watched out of the corner of her eye as Alice reached for her hanging pocket and began to pull gently at the draw string, trying to surreptitiously get her hand inside. She had been wondering, before the fellows had set upon them, whether Alice was at the tree because she had made the charm offering Marjorie had suggested to her a few moons back… Seeing her secrecy now, she suspected that the Mistress still had the charm upon her. And she would be right to be worried. If they found it about her person, it would only add weight to her guilt. Having some sport with the mistress, Marjorie crept up close beside her, shimmying quietly along the bench and whispered in her ear…

"And what be that then?"

Alice nearly jumped out of her bodice.

Annoyed and defensive she replied, "Tis a prayer…" but then looking up at Marjorie's face, she saw that the old woman had guessed what it might be.

Finally untangling the chord, she pulled out the egg and held it up to the light. "I ought to smash this and hide it somewhere," she whispered.

"What be it for?" asked the girl from the floor.

"Twas for the tree," Alice replied briskly, trying to make it plain it was none of the girl's business. Marjorie watched Alice rise and start to hobble about the church, peering into the growing darkness to see where she might safely hide it.

"Asking what?" continued the girl, oblivious to the rebuke.

"That be her business," Marjorie cut in and Alice flashed her a smile. She held out her hand and indicated to Alice that she should give her the egg. At first, Alice hesitated, but with a sharper gesture Marjorie made it clear she should hand the egg over and this time Alice trusted her. Hobbling over, she handed her the charm. Marjorie took it and stowed it deep within her basket, hiding it in amongst the balls of wool. They would find it, of course, when they searched there thoroughly, but she cared not. They would undoubtedly hang her whatever she said or did now. But she might be able to save the other two. Alice thanked her with a weak smile and gave her a little bow of a curtsy, before sitting back down in silence.

By revealing the egg, a kind of confession has been shared between them and Marjorie could not help but think on the conversation she had shared with Alice when the Mistress had come to her and asked for help with her situation. All in the village were aware that she had born Master John no childer, so Marjorie knew what she would be asking for when she appeared at the door to her hovel. In truth, she was surprised it had taken her so long. She had told the Mistress to do two things: One was to make the egg charm and to bury it in a place that felt sacred to her. The second was to feed her fellow plenty of meat, mushrooms and beans. The priests were always happy to point the finger at the Mistress for being barren, but as a midwife, Marjorie could see plainly that this was not always the truth of it. From what she knew of this woman's Master John, his eyes were often wandering. Yet none of the maids he had ever wandered too had fallen with child either. The other fellows in the village thought him lucky, apart for in his choice of wife. But Marjorie suspected otherwise.

When she told Alice to bury the egg somewhere sacred, she had not expected it to be at the same tree and at the same time as she was about her business. Marjorie came here every year to this tree at Beltane, to gather her properties, as it was on this day that their potency was at their strongest.

The yew tree had been known as a symbol of long life and rebirth since days of old. There were many scattered across the country that had been worshipped since heathen times and then churches had been built beside them. When Marjorie joined the church, her Mother Superior had shown her how to use the bark, branch tips, and needles to make medicines. Despite being poisonous, when used by fools, she knew how to turn each part into a remedy. Some could be used for treating tapeworms, some swollen tonsils. Parts could be used for treating seizures, muscle aches, pain when pissing, and with women, parts of it could be used for bringing on the monthly flow and abortions. Many mistresses had come to the nuns for such things in those days, and the nuns had the protection of the church should anyone find out, even though it had been against the laws of the church to do such things… But each convent and monastery had their own rules and secrets.

"This cannot be smashed," announced the young maid suddenly from over by the altar, rousing Marjorie from her thoughts.

Taken aback, she peered over at the girl, who was standing holding out what, in the gloom, looked like a folded piece of paper.

"And what be that then?" she asked her…

∞

As the train pulls out of Brighton Station, in the direction of Lewes, the sun comes bursting through the window, shining brilliant rays of golden light through the panes of glass, bathing my face in a warm glow. I purposefully sat on the west side of the train, so I could watch the sun setting on route to the play.

Opposite me is a pretty curvy lady who is also enjoying the warmth of the sun on her skin. I wonder whether she knows she has sat on the west side of the train too. She is clearly having a lovely time with the light hitting her face. Breathing in deeply, right down to my feet, I close my eyes and my heart rate drops. I smile. I am so very glad to be here. Everything feels… right. I love this time of day. It is my favourite kind of light… The 'golden hour'.

Across from us, on the neighbouring set of seats, is a stunningly beautiful young lady, short hair, elfin featured, with a hoodie on and headphones in. She has her feet up on the opposite seat and is scrolling through her phone, in that bored nonchalant way that young people have mastered so effortlessly.

I can't shake the feeling that I'm returning to something… The tree maybe? Perhaps I've seen that tree somewhere before, but the only yew trees I've come across recently have been in the forest of Kingley Vale and the one in my vision was solitary. Obviously, I've seen lots of solitary yew trees in churchyards over the years… I open my eyes and take out my phone to Google 'churchyard yew trees'. It takes a moment for the images to load, and I allow myself time to sit back and close my eyes again as the heavy sunlight cuts slices across my eyes as houses and trees block its view from me. After a moment, I check the uploaded images. And there it is… On the first page, the yew tree I had seen in my vision. It does not have ribbons hanging from it and it is held up with walking sticks and chains, looking older and wider than the one I'd seen, but it is undeniably the same tree. I click on the website and read that the yew tree is 1600 years old, planted in 400 AD and the church next to it was built in the 1100's, which means the tree came first. I've read before how many churches were built in places that were sacred already and that many churches have yew trees in their churchyards that are older than the buildings. Then I see that this tree is in the churchyard of St Mary's Church in Wilmington! Oh Kairos! This means of course that I can go and have a look at it tonight, if I have the chance. Perhaps I have been to it before then, as a little girl? I resolve to ask my mother when I check in on her next week…

∞

I'm feeling anxious and sort of excited. That guy, the fucking jester, or whatever he was, really got under my skin. I didn't fancy him… He has a cock for a start, but it's that kind of feeling. He seemed like trouble. In a fun way. Not in a like-my-asshole-brother kind of way. And somehow, within a matter of seconds and in the middle of the coffee shop, he manged to get out of me that I could get hold of some weed and mushrooms. I don't even know why I told him that. I was kind of showing off. I was also high. But then he asked me if I could get him some for tonight, and I agreed! Now, somehow, I'm on a fucking train going to Wilmington, with a pocket full of mushrooms and an ounce of skunk, which I can clearly smell through my bag, even though I wrapped it in a ton of cling film and buried it deep within my stinking work clothes.

There's an old woman opposite me. She's on her phone and looks like she's way too old to know what the smell of weed is. Then there's a middle-aged woman across from her who looks like she's had a spliff or two in her time, so should be no sweat.

Watching the old woman using her phone is kind of jokes. I always think it looks funny seeing old people using smartphones. I know it shouldn't, but it just seems like it doesn't fit somehow. Like smartphones are cutting edge and old people are like, well… Old. My mum always has a go at me about how much I'm on my phone. My arm does ache the whole time from RSI, and I can kind of feel it's giving me depression. But I'm on meds for that anyway and I can't function without a phone. It's literally my most important possession.

The middle-aged woman across from me is looking at her phone too and then she starts giggling, and I wonder what she's found so funny. I look past her and out the window to the sunset. It's beautiful. It's doing that rich red-light bit it does just before it goes all pink and blue. Matt will be down at the beach right now with all our mates. I keep wondering if I'm making a mistake, going all the way to Wilmington to meet this guy, but he didn't look like a serial killer, I mean he'd be a pretty bloody conspicuous serial killer if he is one, which would actually be quite smart. But I don't care and I'm skint. He ordered £100 of mushrooms and an ounce of weed. Matt sorted out a sweet deal for me, which means I'm getting a free ten bag out of both deals. Matt thought I was mad for going, but I was up for getting out of the city for the night. The guy had given me a flyer to see his play and invited me to the after party, so I knew he was legit, and the venue where the play and party are taking place is infamous for having some banging nights… So I'm in. I was hoping that Matt would come with me, but he'd already arranged to hook up with the guy from last night again. I decided not to cock block him and make like a grown up.

∞

My husband has sent me a funny gif of a kitten riding on the head of a Great Dane and it's made me giggle out loud. I love the gifs he sends me. Gifs are like modern day bunches of flowers. Shows he's thinking of me. I do love him, the great oaf. I put the phone down on my lap and sit back again to enjoy the sun light. It's just beautiful right now, that gorgeous view of Brighton you get as you're pulling out of the station is one of my favourite views of the city. As we travel over the large old viaduct I smile out over the rooftops. We pass Moulsecoombe and the sun keeps bursting through intermittently, until we hit the South Downs and the views are just stunning… Rolling fields like giant breasts, shimmering in the light as if draped in golden chiffon… But as we pull into Falmer my heart sinks. Both platforms, on either side of the tracks, are lined with men. The football has just finished. Seagull's fans are hollering at Southend fans all along the stretch of the station. A man in a Hi-Vis vest is trying desperately to keep the men back safely behind the yellow line, but the guys are dancing, swearing and shouting… and yes, pulling moonies. As we grind to a halt, the men on our side of the tracks spill in through the opening carriage doors. They're shouting and jeering "come on then!" and "you're still going down!" The older woman opposite me is on it and calls over to the younger girl to come and join us in our set of seats, but she takes too long to register what the woman is saying and is suddenly surrounded by a loud jeering crowd. It seems like there's millions of them. Every seat gets filled and every inch of the aisles are full. A father and his little girl thankfully sit down next to the older woman, and the two seats next to me are occupied by an older couple, both sporting their team's scarf and cap. But the young woman across from us is surrounded by red-faced, middle-aged men, all leaning over her to get to the window, their attention directed towards the Seagull fans on the opposite platform. Everyone on all sides is shouting obscenities and swearing blue murder at each other… Whilst also flashing their fat spotty arses. The little girl opposite me turns to her dad and asks him,

"Why are they allowed to swear at us like that, Daddy?"

I don't catch his answer, because at that moment the doors beep and begin to close. The train pulls away.

All the men, who no longer have anyone to shout abuse at, notice that there are other people in the carriage. Behind me, I hear one of them standing by the door, shout to the young lady across from us, who his mate has sat down next to,

"be careful sitting next to him love, he just got out of prison... For rape!" he jeers, and all the men around him start laughing.

The bloke next to her shouts at him to shut up, but the guy at the door continues,

"Don't worry though love, it was with a little boy."

I look at the older woman opposite me and she shakes her head with contempt. The guy at the door catches sight of the look on her face.

"Cor, she's fit, in't she?" he shouts sarcastically to his mate sitting across from us, and the guy turns towards the woman and me, eyeing us up like lamb chops, drawing his own conclusions, though he does not reply.

"What about that one?" the guy at the door shouts. I guess he's indicating to me as he can only see the back of my head. "Is she alright?"

Most of the carriage are now weighing us up, whilst also pitying us for having caught the scumbag's attention.

I look out the window, to show that I'm ignoring him. They continue to shout, swear and chant as I look at the beautiful rolling downs. I close my eyes against the sun as it hits my face once more and try to block out the thuggish voices ricocheting around me.

∞

I wish I'd joined the other two women before this lot got on, but I'm stuck here now. God, I fucking hate guys like this. It's not even football fans, it's certain types of football fans. Assholes who think that when there's a bunch of them drunk together, they can suddenly fuck off all manners and treat everyone like shit. I mean what the fuck... Why is this shit sociably acceptable?

There's a guy shouting something at me, but I've turned up the volume on my music so I can't hear him.

Wankers.

Outside, the rolling hills are turning pink and in the dips between, there's a greeny blue mist. I watch as a bunch of birds fly past, heading towards the sunset disco at the pier. I think of the starlings that do that cool flying formation thing over the West Pier and I suddenly really wish I hadn't left Matt and the others. They'd be watching the birds and drinking vodka from the bottle right now. If I was there with them, I would not be currently surrounded by beer-breathed meat heads. Eurgh. The worst thing is, I took another mushroom just before I got on the train. Hope they're all gone before *that* starts to kick in…

∞

It is unfortunate that the cast of Planet of the Apes have cared to join us, for what was otherwise proving to be a lovely train journey. I smile at the little girl who has sat down next to me with her father. She is clearly a little disturbed by the high stimulation of everything going on around her and doesn't understand why it is okay for everyone to be behaving like animals. And to this I have no answer.

"Was that your first game?" I peer over her father to ask her.

She shakes her head shyly, and her father answers for her.

"She's been a couple of times before, haven't you hun?" but she wriggles behind his arm.

"That was her biggest match though," he continues.

"And did you win?" I ask, smiling at her dad, but then looking directly at her.

The girl shakes her head. She looks down and starts playing with her scarf.

"Oh, that's a shame," I sympathise. Appreciating now why the train is feeling so aggravated, and why the men on the other platform were being so provocative.

"Is that a new scarf?" I ask, changing the subject.

She nods.

We pull into Lewes station, and thankfully, many of the supporters get off the train. There's still enough to be annoying, but the frenetic energy that such a crowd creates significantly thins. One of the seats across from us becomes free and the awful man who had previously been shouting at the door comes over and sits down to be closer to his friend. They're both carrying white flimsy carrier bags full to almost breaking point with cans of cheap larger. Taking out a fresh can and cracking it open, he starts to check out the plump woman sat across from me, who he had not been able to see the face of before and then he looks at me. I hold his gaze until he sneers. He breaks away and decides to size up the man next to me instead and evaluates he can goad him by interacting with his daughter, separated from her by just the aisle:

"You out tonight for a beer?" he asks the little girl.

The girl initially shrinks from him, but also finds the question funny.

"You know paper, scissors, stone?" he asks her, and she nods.

"Alright, I'll play you then… Best of three."

She nods excitedly and sits upright to take on the challenge. They play and she wins. They play again and she wins again. Boosting her confidence, she proudly looks around to see who has noticed her victory. The blonde woman opposite me and I beam at her, giving her encouragement and keeping an eye on the man.

"Okay best of five," he says, and let's make it interesting. "I'll bet you for your shirt" he says and pulls at her T-shirt. The little girl recoils and shakes her head vigorously.

"What… Do you think I'll beat you then?" he asks all innocently, but she continues to shake her head.

"Well, what you gonna give me if I win then?" he pushes. She looks up at her dad, who looks down at her with submission in his face, leaving the ball firmly in her court.

The girl withdraws further and so the man tries a different tack.

"You coming to the game next week then?" he asks, reaching out and touching her bare arm. She shakes her head and then thankfully the Dad starts getting up as the train pulls into Glynde.

"I'll see you next week then, yeah?" the man calls to the girl as she alights the train. He turns back around, laughing to himself smugly, before catching sight of me and the woman opposite, both staring at him with utter disdain. Realising that we've been watching his actions and are very much judging him, he turns to his friend and asks;

"Where's Chris?"

"He just texted, he's in the next carriage."

"Come on then," he commands and flicks his hand out, hitting his friend hard on the leg. They get up and leave, grabbing their bags of beer as they go. The ugly cretin leers over us threateningly as he goes. I do not drop my stare from his and look him right in the eye. He snorts and breaks his gaze, as he makes his way to the door. Then shouts back over his shoulder,

"Your milkshake brings all the dogs to the yard!"

I look over at the woman opposite me and we both begin to laugh.

What an imbecile.

∞

I'm relieved as hell when the gross guy gets up and goes to the next carriage with his mate, although I can still hear him shouting next door. At least he's not in here though.

There's still the older couple sat next to me and a younger man left behind, who is sat over by the young woman in the hoodie. And of course, there's the nice older lady sat in front of me, with whom I just shared a giggle. Gosh, that creep made my skin crawl.

The fans begin to make conversation about the game, and I listen in as the younger guy starts chatting to the older couple about today's result…

"In '83 we got through to the final, then we went down."

"Don't say it, just don't even say it, you'll jinx us." the old boy interjects. It makes me laugh the way football fans are so superstitious.

I take out my phone and check to see if my husband has sent me anymore animal-related gifs, but it's blank. I flick about through Facebook and Instagram, but nothing new has happened and there's no notifications, so I switch it off again and stare back out the window. I see the sky has started turning pink and the Downs are now a misty blue. A heron flies across the sunset. Then the hills give way to flat lands and flood plains, glowing now in a rich tapestry of greens, laced with ribbons of brilliant pink shining out brightly as streams intersect the fields, catching the setting light on their still dark waters.

The train pulls into Berwick, the couple and the other chap get off, leaving me and the two women I was on here with originally, alone again. As the doors shut, we all shift in our seats relaxing, visibly relieved that everyone else has gone, even though I only have one more stop to go. But then we hear from the other carriage,

"Does your mother know?"

That guy is still on the train.

The older woman and I laugh. Then we settle back and enjoy the last of the sunset. The woman opposite closes her eyes and I too suddenly feel very tired. The oppressive atmosphere of the last twenty minutes has taken its toll. This play had better be good.

I used to catch lots of trains, back when I was young and single. At one point I had ten lovers on the go who I kept on rotation. I was always catching trains to various parts of the country to visit them. They had all been very special to me and I was very much in love with some of them. Still am really. But none of them had been born with the balls to commit. And struggling to get a man to commit was so very, very dull. When I met my husband, the thing that I liked best about him was his loyalty to his best friend. And then, when he decided, after not much time had passed, that I was the one, he committed straight away. He proposed to me within a matter of weeks. I'd said yes without a moment's hesitation. In many ways, we were not as well matched as I had been with some of my previous lovers, but the fact was he was the one who was up for committing. And I knew he was trustworthy… It just trumped everyone else really.

I notice the train is slowing down and so I open my eyes. The sky is mottled in pale pinks and blues, turning everything into one big milkshake.

The train slowly grinds to a halt.

Out of the window I can see a little muddy lake, with a roost of crows in the trees, reflecting perfectly as mirrored silhouettes on the water's surface.

As above, so below… I think to myself.

After a minute the loudspeaker announces; *this is your driver speaking. I'm sorry to inform you there is going to be a severe delay to this evening's journey. I've just been told that a tree has fallen onto the tracks up ahead. Engineers are being called to the scene and will clear it away as soon as possible, but we will be here for the foreseeable. I'm sorry for any inconvenience this may have caused.*

I audibly groan and the men in the next carriage start shouting aggressively… *You're kidding me! What the FUCK!*

Bollocks… I think to myself. *Everything I try to do! The universe is always out to stop me…*

If I had been on my own, I would have punched something. Possibly my own face. I've found myself doing that quite a lot recently.

∞

Oh no, oh no, oh no, oh no…. Please, please, please! I cannot get stuck on this fucking train! I'm starting to feel that other mushroom kick in.

I'm having a panic attack, I'm panicking. I'm having a panic attack. I look out the window so that no one can see my fear. My psychiatrist taught me to slowly breathe in for a count of three, hold it for three, and then breathe out for three. I'm doing it. I don't know how I remember, but I'm doing it. The terror starts to subside… I let myself breathe normally again.

I lean my head back on the chair and kick my feet up onto the seat opposite in a huff, clenching my fists in fury. I'd timed it all so perfectly, so I'd be coming up just as I started watching the play. I mean, if I've got to watch theatre… Fuck. For fuck's sake. I'm going to be totally fucked soon…

I feel such an idiot. I wish I'd never come. This was a stupid idea. I should never have left the city.

I stare out the window and see a bunch of rabbit's sprinting across the field beside me. Looking up to see what's shocked them, I spot bird of prey swooping up into a tree. For a moment it takes the edge off. Can't remember the last time I saw a bird of prey. That's pretty neat actually…

∞

"Tis a curse," Kitty told the old woman, holding out the folded-up piece of paper in her outstretched hand. She could not believe she was showing this to them, but she had been thinking on how she must get rid of it before the men returned. And if the old woman had been willing to take the egg, then perhaps she would take this one too…

…But the old woman was laughing at her.

"Then wherefore be it upon a piece of paper?" she snorted.

"I know not how to make one." Kitty replied indignantly, "I read about them in my father's library."

Now the old woman was *really* tickled.

"In thy father's library!" she roared, suddenly enlivened by the whole situation, "Thou trespassed in thy father's library to learn how to make a curse? What… Thou found it in a book or some such?"

"Thy father has books on curses?" asked the plump one, looking ever so shocked at the news. Kitty suddenly wondered if this woman knew her father, and therefore knew who she was too.

"It 'was not in a book, it 'was on some papers…" she went on, but the old woman was not listening, still snorting with laughter. “So, is this what they be writing about in books these days?”

The old woman turned to the other one and said in earnest, “There was a time when they’d just come knock on my door,” then she turned back to Kitty and asked “When did thou get thy letters? Here, let me look…”

Kitty had not caught up with all that the old woman had said, who was a spritely thing despite her many years, and she did not have time to reply before Marjorie snapped at her,

“Well? I can’t hear thee?”

“Since I had eight summers,” Kitty retorted. She was not used to being spoken to this way, “my father had us schooled.”

“Who be it cursing?” asked the plump one, who had taken the paper out of the old woman’s hand and was turning it about, trying to make sense of it. Obviously neither of the women had their letters. Kitty considered lying to them, but then thought the old one would probably be able to tell and would not help her if she thought she was lying.

“My father,” Kitty confessed.

Now that really made the old woman choke with mirth.

"Thou art cursing thy father, from a book found in his library?" she guffawed, slapping her thighs merrily. Kitty began to worry that she might attract the guards.

She whispered, "It was on some papers in the library. I did find them bound up in a leather cover, up upon the highest shelf. I think mayhap they were my mother's… "

That stopped them in their tracks.

"Oh…" the old woman pondered thoughtfully. "She was a sweet thing…"

"In truth?" Kitty asked, her interest piqued, "I do not remember her."

"Aye," the old woman recalled, "When she clapped eyes on thee, she was."

Kitty went over to the old woman and knelt at her feet, looking up eagerly.

"There thou wert," the old woman continued, "Squiggly little thing… Couldn't wait to be in the light. Thou was the first, but thou was fast. No more than two hours in the bearing. And thy blessed mother beamed when she laid eyes on upon thee, as if thou wert a fresh May morn."

Kitty could not believe her ears. This was not the story her father had told her, and her eyes began to well up. She fought hard to keep back the tears.

"I did not know that," she whispered.

"Well I remember it well. I liked thy mother. She was a sweet thing."

∞

Alice looked down at the young maid and could see she had tears in her eyes. It was quite a thing, Alice considered, how Marjorie knew the story of how all the folks in the village came into the world. And how they all left it too, as she was also the one who lay out the dead, being the village death monger and all…

Alice also considered how it must be hard growing up without a mother and suddenly felt a tinge of sympathy for the young woman who had just come and sat at their feet.

What a shame it was, she thought to herself, *that there were women in the world who desperately wanted daughters and daughters who desperately wanted mothers, but God had not had the good sense to put them together. I am old enough to be this maid's mother. She would not have had the fine dresses, but she would have been well loved. And by the looks of things, she would have been the happier for it.*

Suddenly Alice felt very drawn to the maid and wished to hold her in her arms.

Instead she looked down at the curse and said, "this be finely made," though she could not understand what was written upon it.

"Little good that will do me upon the morrow," answered the girl bitterly.

Alice found she could not bear the thought of anything happening to this girl upon the morrow.

"Wherefore art thou cursing thy father?" Marjorie asked.

The girl looked down at her pale hands for some time, considering what to tell the women, then looked up and said;

"He was to force me to marry. For this reason, I did write the curse, to protect myself from him… And… To protect myself from… Others."

Alice looked over at Marjorie and saw she had heard it too… There was something in the way she had said 'others'.

Marjorie took the curse from Alice's hand and hid it in her basket, along with the egg, much to the young woman's relief.

Alice continued to consider the girl. A young mistress of her standing would not be marrying a fellow for love. Her father would be choosing a husband for her. And knowing Will, her father, his choice in husband would have little to do with his daughter's happiness and everything to do with clambering up the social ranks. Looking at the maid, Alice could see she was full of shame, and this broke Alice's heart.

Suddenly Alice confessed, "No childer will come for me as I have no childer. That be what I was doing at yonder yew tree."

∞

Kitty looked up at the plump woman and smiled. No one had ever confided in her before. Something inspired Kitty to lift her hand up, and as she did so, the woman reached out too. Suddenly they were holding hands. They sat together in silence for some moments, the whole time Kitty's body was on fire at the feeling of their touch. The woman too seemed to be overcome with the moment, but after a while they grew awkward and she dropped Kitty's hand, announcing,

"I doth need a drink."

To which the older woman slapped the plump one's thigh, making her yelp, as it was her bad leg, and retorted,

"There! Now that be the first sensible thing, thou hath said since we got here."

"Will there be wine?" asked the plump one.

"Aye," replied the older woman. "There will be wine…"

She leant into the other woman's face and whispered, "there will be the blood of Christ."

The plump one looked back at her and smiled "I wish greatly to drink of the blood of Christ!"

Kitty laughed nervously. That was possibly the most blasphemous thing anyone had ever said in the whole of Christendom.

"Thou can come help too young maid," the older woman commanded her. "Thems that don't look, don't get."

Kitty rose nervously to her feet and began to help them.

∞

Peering about into the darkness, Marjorie searched the church recesses for where the wine might be stored. It had originally been kept in a cabinet beside the alter, back in the days of the Eucharist, but Marjorie did not know if it would still be kept there. She stepped up towards the cabinet and gave it a pull. It was locked. She turned back to find Alice was also hobbling her way towards to the cabinet. They looked at each other and Marjorie rattled the latch again to show Alice it was fastened.

"I can pick locks..." came the young woman's voice.

This took Marjorie by surprise...

"Was that learnt in the library too then?" she smirked.

"Was learnt getting into the library," the young shrew curtsied.

∞

They all sniggered at her coquettishness and stepped back so she could have the light. Pulling a pin from her coif, the girl set about twisting and turning inside the mechanism of the lock. Alice stood about for a moment with Marjorie, but her leg soon began to throb, so she returned to the bench. Her eyes fell back to the door. John should have been here by now, if he was planning to come. The sun was setting, painting orangey reds across the sky. There had been more than enough time for the fellows who had forced them into the church to go back to the green and for word to have spread to all those concerned. And then beyond… Everyone would have heard about what had happened by now.

Why has John not come for me? Alice screamed in her head.

He had not come back to the cottage after the service. She had eaten her victuals on her own, looking across at the empty space to the opposite side of the board where he should have sat. She made her own way down to the festivities with a heavy heart, but when she had got there, she found that he was very busy. The fire had been allowed to go out beneath the hog during the church service (the Masters of the Green had obviously been spending too much time guarding the ale and not enough time taking any heed to the other matters at hand), so John had been asked to go down to the Bakery and fetch up his bellows. He'd been there tending to the fire ever since and had not had time to return to the cottage. That was all. When he had seen Alice, he had scooped her up at the waist and given her a big kiss, wishing her a happy Beltane. Then he had asked her to fetch him some ale. She had gone to the barrels, but Marigold had been there, and she had not liked the way the wench had looked at her. She'd gone back and given John his flagon of ale, then joined her friends; Hannah, a practical and red-headed chandler, and Lettys the potter, who was very fond of laughing and merriment, over on the benches by the green. The women had all been friends since they were babes. They talked of small things, gossiping about the folks that fell across their gaze, whilst they shared a cup or two of ale. The Maypole dancing started, and they cheered and clapped along. Alice would have loved to dance the Maypole. She always used to in her younger years, but she was too old for all that now. If she fell and hurt herself, then she would not be able to work, which would mean they would not be able to eat. Such merriment was for younger folks with youthful bones; with nothing on their minds but courting. She had looked over again at the hog and had seen Marigold there, laughing and flirting with the men, including John, who glanced at Alice, as if he had been checking to see she wasn't looking. Their eyes had met. He had smiled at her warmly though and she had wondered if it was all just in her head. He was a friendly soul and Alice's jealousy had vexed him before, so she did not want him to think that she did not trust him. That was when she had risen and made her way towards the tree. She thought that if he saw her smiling and leaving him to it, then it would look as if she trusted him. Which she did…

Suddenly the young maid blurted,

"Whatever happens to us upon the morrow, it will be better than being sold off to some vile master."

"If thou sees thy father upon the morrow," Alice replied conspiratorially, "thou should shout thy curse at him. It will put the fear of god into him."

The girl went back to picking the lock, her face full of thoughts.

"What will they do to us upon the morrow?" she asked.

Alice looked over at the cunning woman for an answer.

"I think there will be a trial," the old woman replied.

At this, the women both turned and looked at her. Alice had been so busy in her own thoughts of John she had not stopped to imagine that such a thing would be in the making. Suddenly she felt less keen for the door to swing open.

"A trial?"

"Will my father be there?" asked the girl.

"Aye," Marjorie nodded. "I should think all the folks from the village will be."

"Thinks thee that your husband will be there?" the girl asked Alice…

And Alice found that she was full of rage.

"My husband better be there," she fumed, struggling to her feet and limping towards the great wooden door, "If he will let them chasten me in front of the whole village, then he better bloody be there. I will look him right in the eye."

"And thinks thee my sisters will come?" the girl whimpered.

Alice did not notice the breaking in the girl's voice, and carried on with her fury, raging at the door.

"Oh aye, they'll make all the women of the village come watch. We all had to go watch Mary Childcraft…" She crowed, swinging around, before finally seeing Marjorie's face, fervently indicating to Alice the girl's distress. Realising the effect she was having, Alice let out her breath, and took herself back to the bench; lowering herself down heavily with indignation.

“And how did they know we would be here?” asked the girl, confused.

“They knew she would be here…” Alice cut in, glaring over at Marjorie.

“If they wished to come for me, they would have knocked down my door…” Marjorie protested.

“They had to catch thee in some ungodly act!” Alice insisted “All about the village knew that thou would be up here doing something to this here yew tree at some point over Beltane. All they had do was sit and wait for thee.”

This made the old woman angry.

“I’ve been visiting this sacred yew tree every bleedin’ festival since Abraham was born,” she snapped.

“Aye!” Alice retorted, “so they knew that thou would be here.”

They all fell into a bubbling silence.

∞

Oh Kairos, what work will you have me do here then?

I open my eyes when I hear the announcement and look around the carriage. The woman opposite is looking about the train in that funny way the English do when they're trying to help or do something about the situation but are just covering up their fear of having lost control. She is a small blonde lady with short hair. She looks sassy and yet also deeply sad. Anxious even. I'm worried about her. It doesn't quite fit together. She is clearly confident and has an extrovert dress sense, but something about her looks utterly vulnerable. Broken somehow.

I take a glance at the young girl sitting on the seats across the aisle. Her leg has just begun to shake anxiously. She is staring out the window, giving off some strong 'don't talk to me' signals. Well… That's never stopped me.

I check and am relieved to see there is a toilet at the other end of the carriage, which is otherwise empty. It's just us left in here, apart from the awful men on the other side of the door. My bladder is not as strong as it used to be, and I drank a bottle of wine at my god daughter's house this afternoon. Not on my own, obviously…

My god daughter is now nineteen. She is the daughter of Jo, a woman I used to teach with at drama school. I had been one of the few people invited to Jo's wedding when she married Rob and it had been a deep honour to then be asked to be their daughter's God Mother. She was a miracle baby. She had appeared suddenly and naturally after Jo and Rob had spent many years trying IVF. And when she was little, she had been the sweetest thing. The most sparkly soul. I love being her God Mother. I taught her how to be a magical fairy and how to cast spells on flowers to help them grow and had knitted her a fabulous fairy cloak, woven out of pinks and whites, all interwoven with glittery threads. It had included one black fake rose sewn on at the neck. Because, although she was currently a fairy, one day she too would become a witch. She is now in her wilderness years and I hope my presence as a God Mother is helping her as a guiding light. It is so hard for young people growing up these days to navigate their way through the obstacles of life, especially when bloody social media lies across their path, like a tree on the tracks. I had been shown my God Daughter's Instagram account by a concerned Jo. It was all pouting photos of the sweet girl we both know and love, flaunting her half naked body and getting drunk with equally orange and duck faced friends. But this was their world now. And one they have inherited from us, their foremothers. Each and every one of us adults, all across the world, share a responsibility for the future that now lies before our fledgling daughters. And it does not look like it is going to be pretty. I'm rather glad I won't be around for the shit show that's brewing.

I glance back over at the young girl across from us and think that it is no wonder they all look so despondent. And no wonder they generally have very little interest in our advice. All we have done for them is screw everything up.

For the twentieth time that day, I thank the Goddess I don't have children.

∞

I reach down and check to see if I have any water. I take out a plastic bottle from my bag and shake it. It's only a third full, which makes me let out an involuntary and audible huff of frustration.

"I've got plenty" says the older woman.

I look up and see she is smiling at me and already beginning to rummage around in her bag. She is an attractive lady, with wild greying used-to-be-blonde hair and piercing eyes; so hazel they are almost golden. Especially in this light. They look completely orange, but for a thin ring of brilliant green around the edges. She wears bright red lipstick and an equally bright red scarf around her neck. Otherwise she is completely dressed in black. She cuts quite the dramatic figure. Which I like. I want to be something like this when I grow up.

"Thank you," I respond, taken aback by the generosity and not wanting to put the woman out. "I have a little for now, but that's good to know." I say, shaking the bottle.

"Well let's hope we won't be stuck in here for long," she smiles, "but if you run out…"

From her handbag she extracts a large black metal water container, which she shakes, and I can hear it is full. She places it on the floor between us.

That is very nice of her, I think to myself and smile again as I sit back, able to now relax, and rebuking myself for cursing the universe. It seems as if it has sent me a guardian angel.

Then the woman continues to rummage and suddenly pulls out a bottle of rioja.

"I've also got this too!" she beams.

I laugh. This is my kind of woman. Although, of course, I'm not drinking…

"Thanks, but I can't. I'm…" I decide to just tell her, "I'm in the middle of doing IVF, so I can't drink."

"Oh!" the woman responds, then thinks and says "Nonsense… I know someone who was recommended by her doctor to go home and get drunk when she was doing IVF. To help her relax. I bet you probably could really do with a drink. And we might be stuck on here for ages…"

She was right. I *really* could do with a drink.

"I've also got three bottles of Longman's Ale in my bag too; in case we still haven't set off by the time we finish this."

I look down the aisle in front of me and then backwards, to check to see if there's a toilet. I don't want to drink any booze on a train without a toilet close to hand, but I see there is one behind me, just before the door to the next carriage. I also notice that no one else is in the carriage, so I feel like fate is telling me to have a glass. I don't mind talking to strangers, but I prefer it when other strangers aren't listening. There is the girl across from us of course, but she has her earphones in and is staring intently out the window. I turn back to the older woman and smile in acknowledgement that a spot of wine would certainly make the current situation much more bearable.

The woman goes back into her bag and produces a round plastic disc, which she unscrews, opens and then flicks out, revealing that it is, in fact, a portable telescopic champagne flute. I laugh.

"It was my birthday in March and I only just caught up with my God Daughter," the woman explains. "This little set is a birthday present from her."

She unscrews the bottle, pours a splash of wine into the cup, testing it to see if it leaks. Seeing that it doesn't, she continues to pour a little more in.

"Oh," I respond, "Well then, happy birthday."

I take the glass from her outstretched hand and toast the older woman and take a sip. It tastes glorious and I can feel it going straight to my head. The woman then proceeds to extract a tupperware box filled with nuts and a packet of dates. She opens these up and offers them to me. Smiling, I take a nut and hand the glass back.

Then she shouts over to the girl across from us to see if she wants any, but the girl, pulling out an earphone for a moment, shakes her head furiously and puts it back in. She looks like she's pissed off with the whole situation, which I understand, but we might as well make the most of it, seeing as there's nothing we can do about it.

The older woman is unperturbed, and drinks down a sip of the rejected wine, sighing with deep satisfaction. She smiles into the cotton candy light, with her eyes closed in pleasure. I enjoy her calmness. This woman clearly has her shit together.

I look back out the window too. A black crow is sitting eyeing me suspiciously from a nearby tree.

∞

I had turned the music off on my phone to listen to the announcement and am now listening to the two women chatting. I hate talking to strangers and it does my head in the way old people think they can just talk to whoever they like. The older one offered me some wine and my sphincter shrivelled at the thought of it. I'm jealous of the wine, but I don't know where they've been. I turn to look out of the window, making it clear I'm not fucking interested. But fuck sitting here sober. I've already spotted where the toilet is, in case I need to make a dash for it when the conductor comes, but as the driver just did the announcement, I now know there isn't a conductor on this train, so I can relax. Which means I can do a pipe. I'm up for feeling this mushroom now, if I'm going to be stuck here for ages and they're going to get drunk at me...

I scoop up my bag and make my way towards the toilet. I look down the carriages and see there is that guy from earlier in the next one, along with a bunch of mates. This is annoying. If it had been empty then I'd have gone and sat in there, but I ain't going anywhere near that guy. No thank you. I look down the other end of our carriage and see it's blocked off. We're at the end of the train, which means the driver is nowhere nearby. That's handy but does mean I'll have to go back and sit with those two cronies. Oh well, at least they ain't going to sexually harass me.

I squeeze into the toilet and put my bag up on the sink, which instantly triggers the tap and water begins to spill everywhere.

"SHIT!" I pull my bag out the way and try to brush it off as quickly as I can. The water has already gone all over the place though. "Oh bollocks" I mutter to myself and reach deep into the bag, pulling out the package of weed. I'll have to just put it in my pocket now, but I don't care. If there is no conductor, then those women have no one to report me to. Besides, they don't look like they'd grass.

I pull out my silver bullet and unscrew one end and tap the old ash out into the sink. I place the tip on the side, then begin unwrapping the cling film, regretting wrapping it up so well. Taking out my grinder from my other pocket, I place a dollop of weed in between the spokes, sandwich the grinder together and turn it this way and that, breaking the weed up into smaller and smaller pieces. Opening it up and tapping it, I catch all the weed on one side and set about picking out the now fine dust and begin packing it down into the open end of the bullet. Screwing the tip back on, I take out my lighter and light the tip, sucking down deep on the other end, making it whistle, until a plume of sweet skunk smoke enters my lungs. I've been smoking weed since I was seven. My mum and dad, when they were still together, taught me to skin up so that I could roll up for them. And when I'd asked if I could have a puff, they'd let me. They and their mates thought it was funny to see me doing it. I'd been the first kid in my school to take drugs, by a long way. I was the first kid to be smoking even. It meant the bullies left me well alone, which was amazing really seen as I was expressing gay tendencies from early on and didn't dress like a girlie girl. No one could deny the coolness of a rebel though. And I was the most rebellious kid in the year and basically the whole school, so I nailed that one.

I hold down the smoke for as long as possible, so that nothing will be exhaled.

And it works. When I breathe out the air is clear. And the bullet, of course, lets out no smoke, and doesn't get hot, so I pop it straight back in my pocket. Job done. And that triggers the mushroom nicely. Thank you very much. I unclick the door and make my way back into the carriage. I throw myself down in the set of seats behind the other women, so they can't look at me. I place my ear buds back in my ears and reach into my pockets for my phone, but before I can press play, I catch their conversation…

"I've always wanted a daughter," the middle aged one says. "I'm from a long line of really lovely mothers. My mum, Nan and great Nan were all alive until I was fifteen, which is when my Nan died. I was eighteen when my great Nan died. So, my upbringing was pretty much matriarchal. And they were all utterly lovely women."

Lucky old you, I think, sarcastically.

"You're lucky," answers the older woman, making me smirk. It's like she just read my mind. "I have a very difficult relationship with my mother."

"She's still alive?" asks the other one.

"Yes, she is. My sister and I look after her. And she's hard work," the woman stresses. "Yesterday the girl bringing my Mum's breakfast forgot the milk. When I arrived with my sister, my Mum was in the process of writing a formal letter of complaint. And she got her milk, the girl just forgot it. But she went straight back to the kitchen to go get it for her. So, it was just, you know… A little late. We said to her; *this is a person who is willing to wipe your arse when you've had a shit. So how about you don't send her away for the weekend having received a formal complaint?* She just doesn't get it…"

I hear the woman sit back in her seat exasperated and repeat to herself, "She just doesn't get it."

I think about my Mum… I love that woman so bloody much and wish with all my heart she would stop drinking. But I can't make her do it. She wants to stop, and she at least tries. My loser dad doesn't even get that far. He's currently homeless for fuck sake. But she's still an addict and I don't know if she'll ever really stop being one. I want her to, but I don't hold out much hope.

"Yeah, I didn't realise how unusual it was to get on with your Mum until fairly recently," admits the other woman. "I can't even imagine not getting on with my Mum. She's everything to me. I can't imagine what it must be like to not have that."

"It's tough," the older one sighs and takes a big swig of the wine.

No shit, I think. I have been forced to play mother to my own Mum for the whole of my life. And my Dad. And sort of my Brother too, but he hates it when I mother him. The idea of a Mum looking after me... Or of anyone looking after me... It's literally something I can't get my head around. Like a fucking fairy tale or something.

"You would like to have a little girl then?" asks the older one.

"Yes. I'd like to keep this line of wonderful women going... Feels like it's something that's needed in the world."

∞

The foolish wench had driven Marjorie into a fury. Her work with the yew tree had not been heretical. It was simply that Beltane was the best time for harnessing the yew tree's powers. Every healer worth their salt knew that. As the moon had just been full, she had been collecting the bark and needles, whilst the sap was still pulled up into its extremities. The men knew to find her here, that was all. They'd been shouting at her about business she did not understand, when they had set upon them. Something to do with Anne... They'd said she was dead. Marjorie blessed her soul. She hoped with all her heart it was not true. Anne had been a good friend to Marjorie, since she'd first come to the village, nearly two-score years ago, begging and destitute. Anne had helped her to secure a hovel, vouching for her with the old Lord Goodwin, who had let her reside on his land, in her little hovel, for a small rent.

Nat had been the one kicking up a fuss, probably because his wife had finally had the good sense to stand up to him. That bastard would rather see Marjorie dance upon a rope than lift a finger to help his poor wife? *Well Saint Peter will see thee answers for your sins,* Marjorie thought in anger.

But if Anne was truly dead and they were being accused of murder... Well that was a serious charge. Whichever way the judgement fell it would make a heavy business. If they were not found guilty of Anne's death, then Master Nat would be hung for wrongful accusation, it being a crime punishable by death to wrongfully accuse another of witchcraft, which Marjorie suspected they were being accused of. And that would leave Mistress Abys widowed, with a new babe in arms, grieving a husband she deeply loved and her unable to work. She would be destitute, and the babe would likely perish… Too much ale and hot heads had been the cause of such fuss and sorrow in the world. Marjorie sighed in anger at it all. Stupid men and their stupid weak ways. Messing up the lives of others, all over the earth, all the bloody time.

∞

Kitty was still trying to pick the lock, but her pin only just reached the latch and it was hard to keep it gripped between her fingers whilst lifting the heavy metal. But she did not like to hear the other women bicker, so she worked on, trying to reach the wine quicker, so she might distract them from their quarrelling… She did not like to hear cross words, having grown up hearing her own father often flying into a rage. It set her humours on edge. He had a furious temper and when caught in the wrong place at the wrong time, Kitty had been thrashed with such ferocity, that sometimes she had bled. She could not bear to think of what he would do to her upon the morrow, after the humiliation of a public trial… Being hung or being beaten to death by her father was what she had to look forward to… And neither appealed.

"What if…" she whispered, "What if we should not be here when they come for us upon the morrow?"

"I've been thinking on this," replied the plump one, "but a fellow has been set outside the door and he will hear the window smash in the breaking."

"Nay, I mean… Not here, not here…" she urged and stared at the woman hard, until she grasped her meaning.

"Thou doth mean…"

"Aye" Kitty suggested, "Make it quick."

The plump one took in a sharp breath.

"Doth thou know how to make it quick?" the plump one asked the older woman.

"Aye…" the older one answered, not looking up from her spinning.

"And does thou have the means?" the plump one pressed on.

The old woman shrugged.

They all paused in silent reflection. After a time, the plump one decided,

"Well that be a fine idea."

"Let us get drunk first," started the old lady, suddenly animated "till we are well within our cups. Then we'll think upon the matter."

With a slap of her thighs, the old woman was up and at the cabinet, stood beside Kitty, urging her on.

Once the woman was looming over her, Kitty found the encouragement she needed to get purchase on the latch and she pinged the lock open, with a satisfying click. There was a round of cheers and the old woman pulled open the doors and reached deep inside its recesses. Extracting a large silver goblet and a full bottle of red wine, she shouted a "Huzzah!" Kitty felt a swell of pride.

"And there be plenty more where that came from!" the old woman announced, indicating to the cupboard.

All their spirits raised. To get through the night warmed with reddish wine was a far better prospect than that of spending slow hours sober and frozen with fear.

∞

"We will have a drop of wine," announced the cunning woman, pouring out a goblet full "And then listen to the good lord's words. That will strengthen our spirits."

Alice was taken aback…

"Thou will have us drink the blood of Christ, whilst we listen to the good Lord's words?" she asked her.

"Aye," she replied sharply, "That be what we are going to do young maid and I'll not have thee stand there looking at me like that with thy hands on thy hips."

"Why would thou wish to hear the good Lord's words? It will be that priest who will have us shamed upon the morrow. Thou doth not believe in him anyway."

"I will thank thee not to tell me what I do and do not believe in," the cunning woman snapped back.

"They have told us to change our minds on what to believe in," Alice went on, unperturbed, "So many times, I know not what way be up nor down no more."

Marjorie ignored her and walked over to the young maid, who had returned to her cushion by the altar. She handed her the goblet…

"Now do I the right thing by giving thee the cup first?" Marjorie asked.

The girl looked over at Alice, who shrugged back at her.

"I know not?" answered the girl.

"Well I do." quipped Marjorie, making her way over to the bench beside Alice, where she sat down heavily and slapped the bench between them. "Now come thou hither and sit thy arse here. With this last precious light, we will hear these words."

And with that, Marjorie reached into her basket and pulled out a battered and well-loved leather-bound book.

Alice was shocked to see a book emerge from the old woman's basket and did not understand at first why she should have one. She did not have her letters...

Taking a deep sip of wine, the girl wiped her mouth on the back of her hand and made her way over to the bench. She sat down between Alice and the cunning woman.

"How taste'th the wine?" asked Alice, fishing for the next sip.

"Better than a fellow," the girl answered.

All three women screamed with laughter, quickly suppressing their noise, so as not to alert the guards outside. Alice thought to herself, *how in God's teeth does she know?* Alice liked a touch of bawdy humour, one could not be married to a fellow like John and not find mirth over a little inn house jollies, if kept within reason, but she had not expected the young maid to come out with something as bawdy as that… It concerned Alice.

Still laughing, Marjorie took the goblet from the girl's hand, much to Alice's displeasure, and replaced it with the book, patting against the hard cover,

"Now, thou hast thy letters," then laughing across at Alice, she whispered, "I know this because she found her curse in a library…" then looking back to the girl she said warmly, "Thou found thy curse in a library!"

The girl laughed too, finally seeing it was rather absurd.

∞

Kitty looked down at the cover of the book. It was worn with use, and in the light, she could not make out any title. She opened it and, with just enough light left from the quickly setting sun, she began to read;

"At this time, I was very sorry and reluctant to die… Tis this the Bible?" she asked, looking up. "I do not recognise the passage."

"Nay, tis not the bible," answered the old woman impatiently, "Tis Julian of Norwich…"

"Who is he?" asked Kitty.

"Not he," hurried the woman, "She…"

"A Mistress?" asked Kitty in awe and began investigating the book.

She could not believe it.

"I have never held a book written by a woman before! I did not even know such a thing existed..."

"Aye," answered the old woman, with a little more patience this time, now Kitty was grasping the significance of the thing. "She was an anchorite."

"Be that one of them women that was bricked up in the church walls?" Kitty asked.

"Nay, not bricked in..." the woman laughed, "Well... She was bricked in, aye, but she retired there from life and gave herself unto the Church of Norwich, through her own choice. And there she spent the rest of her days... Living in its walls."

"And there she wrote a book?" Kitty sighed in full reverence.

"Aye... Now read"

The old woman went to pass the goblet of wine to the plump one at the other end of the bench, but found she had her eyes closed.

"Doth thou want any of this" she smarted, making the other woman jump a little and open her eyes with a start, "Thy feet will swing in the morning, so might as well get this down thee…"

∞

Marjorie instantly regretted her jest, as both women went to ask her what she had meant by it, but before either of them had the chance to make a sound, she slapped the book…

"Go on… Read!" she commanded.

The girl looked over at Alice, whose forehead was now etched in worry, but Marjorie pointed again at the well-thumbed passage and eventually the girl took a breath and began…

"Not because there was anything on earth that I wanted to live for nor because I feared anything…"

"Nay I fear nothing... Nay," interrupted Marjorie, for she did not.

"For I trusted in God"

"I do…" she agreed.

"So, I thought, My Good Lord, may my ceasing to live be to thy glory. Then God bought our Lady into my mind…"

"Now doth thou see?" she started, making the girl lower the book in frustration, "How oft has the priest talked about bringing forth our lady into our mind? Never. He's a bastard. Now carry on."

The girl made a sharp intake of breath at this. She had clearly never heard anyone calling the priest a bastard before. *Well, she best get used to it,* thought Marjorie. *He is a bastard. An utter bastard. And best she admits it…*

"Come on…" Marjorie insisted, tapping the book. The girl searched for her place, flustered, and continued…

"I saw her spiritual and bodily likeness in meek and simple maiden of age, in same bodily form as when she conceived…"

"I hath seen her..." Marjorie interjected excitedly "I hath seen her down at the well. I hath seen her down by the river…"

The girl began to laugh… "Aye, but thou doth speak to birds."

"And thou doth not…" Marjorie retorted, "And which of us be the bigger fool?"

"But tis for why folks talk about thee."

"Thou art the one going about with a curse in thy bodice young maid," piped up Alice suddenly, handing Marjorie back the wine.

"Aye," Marjorie smirked, "From a book. Now keep going…"

"God also showed me part of her wisdom and truth of her soul, so I understood with what reverence she beheld her God. And how reverently she marvelled that he chose to be born of her. A simple creature of his own making. For what made her marvel was that he who was the maker chose to be born of a creature he had made, which moved her to say very humbly to the angel Gabriel "Behold the Handmaid of the Lord!" And this night I really understood that she is greater in worthiness and in all grace than all that God made below her for nothing that is made is above her except the blessed manhood of Christ."

"Amen!" exalted Marjorie, "Then what happens…"

The girl laughed at her, but she cared not; she was excited for the next bit….

"There's little thing that is made that is below our Lady St Mary. God showed it to me as small as if it had been a hazelnut;"

"As small as if it had been a hazelnut" repeated Marjorie, as her point had finally been made. Then proudly she announced "I flew one day..."

"Thou flew?" scoffed Alice.

"Of course, I did," she insisted, "With the birds. And I did see this..."

"Where? Where didst thou fly?" Alice asked incredulously.

"Just above," she persisted, "Over Kingston and back again... For the view..."

"What, as a Mistress, or thou flew as a bird?" asked Alice, annoying Marjorie now.

"I flew as me..."

"And did no one see thee?"

"No folks look at anything around here," she sighed, realising she would have to explain everything she said to these halfwits, for they had no imagination, "Least of all flying things. Least of all flying women who hath gone through the change."

"The change?" asked the younger girl.

"Aye, the change…" Marjorie replied, missing the timbre of the girl's question, "The end of my monthly courses…"

The girl still looked confused and Alice smiled at Marjorie as they both began to dawn….

"Thy courses," Marjorie went on, "that come each month. The blood… Between thy legs."

The girl gasped, "How does thou know of this?"

They could not help but laugh at her…

"How doth I know of…? What has no one had the good sense to tell thee of their meaning?"

"The priest told me it…"

"Thou doth not listen to a word that priest tells thee…" Marjorie snapped, but then seeing the girl's face she softened. In truth, it looked as if no one sensible had spoken to her of her courses, sweet thing. *Rich folks are such fools,* she thought to herself.

"But how doth thou know?" asked the girl, snivelling slightly.

"For we all have them," answered Alice kindly. "They show us we are of child-bearing age."

"And tis what tells thee if thou art with child," added Marjorie. "If the child has taken, then the blood doth not issue forth. If it issues forth…"

"Tis thy heart weeping forth bloody tears from between thy legs," Alice piped up.

"Tis not thy heart that bleeds!" scolded Marjorie, hitting her bad leg; making the poor woman yelp like a kicked dog. She had not meant to hit her so hard. She passed her the wine in way of apology. "Tis the nest of thy womb that issues forth, as there be no egg growing within it to warm. Each moon thy womb makes a new nest."

Both the women looked at her in confusion now.

"The priest said it was a curse," the girl whispered. Utterly embarrassed at the women's talk, which broke Marjorie's heart.

"It is not a curse, it is a blessing," Marjorie went on.

"For some," sighed Alice heavily.

"For all!" she pressed, taking back the goblet…

She held it up to the light. The sky was now awash with deep dark pinks and blues, as the last light disappeared. The yew tree was a black silhouette against the water coloured sky and the reflection of the window in the goblet made it glow an eerie blue.

"Thy womb" she prophesied "is a magic chalice. A bowl of power. Whether it be with child or without child, with its monthly courses or without. My monthly courses have stopped, but it still hath magic."

"Aye… What magic be that then?" asked Alice, with genuine interest.

"Well, it doth make me invisible," she answered.

"Invisible?" Alice mocked, turning incredulous.

"Aye. Since the change, folks about the village can see me not, smell me not, nor hear me not… Unless, in truth, I wish to be seen. Which is not oft. Tis why they could not see me when I flew. But I saw them all right, down there, and I could see all the tiny little lights from the fires. I did not like it much. It was sort of flying and sort of floating. But I remembered her and the hazelnut… But for me it was more like a… Like a walnut."

The two younger women looked at each other, utterly perplexed.

"Listen…" she continued. "The path to a good life, is to keep getting far more from far less. Why, a light breeze on the cheek can, in that very moment, open you up to… Well, to everything. Oft times, I while-away half a day just sitting by a patch of grass looking upon it. Because… Because it is the most beautiful thing I have ever seen. I have a favourite patch of grass I sit by, at top of Windover Hill, where the air tinkles. This grassy patch dances all day long with the flights of tiny blue butterflies, they be called Holly Blues, and little wild bees, all bopping and skipping lightly over all the Wild Carrot flowers, which look like little toadstools of cow parsley, in pinks and whites. In places like this, I can breathe.

∞

Kitty looked out the window in the direction of the hill and thought on how free she had been there, just the night before. *Had it really only been last night?* She could not believe so much had changed in such a short time.

∞

Alice wiped tears from her eyes as she thought on how she might never see another butterfly or smell another flower ever again.

∞

"And all this…" Marjorie continued, waving her arms about her emphatically, "<u>All</u> this… This is <u>all</u> on the hazelnut… Or the walnut."

She flapped at the book again and commanded "read that bit again, thou should listen; tis good."

The girl returned to the book and re-read,

"With this night I really understood that she is greater in worthiness and in fullness of all grace than all that God made below her…"

"And all the men he put between them," spat Marjorie.

"For nothing that is made is above her except the blessed manhood of Christ. There little thing that is made that is below our Lady St Mary, God

showed it to me as small as if it had been a hazelnut…"

"Now doth thou see?" Marjorie insisted, "Jesus, our Lord on Earth, had a Mother… Mary. Do you see? Mary was God's mother on earth. She was his mother. Mary be God's mother…"

The women sat and mulled this over.

"God's Mother…" the girl mused.

"Aye! That priest dwells not much on that part of the bible now does he? Jesus… God, had a Mother… Mary. And all that is below her, which is everything, unto the Lord's greatness and the greatness of his Mother Mary, is as small as if it were a hazelnut… Or a walnut."

She sat back and surveyed them both, to be sure they had finally begun to understand her, and she could see that they had, so she pressed on…

"And that is what it will all look like to us, once they have taken us…"

∞

When the young girl got up to go to the toilet, I asked the blonde lady where she was off to this evening and we'd discovered that both of us were on our way to see the same play! Oh Kairos, I do love thee. And when I asked her how she'd heard about the play, she'd explained that, because she was doing IVF, she'd been rubbing her belly on a maypole for good luck when she'd been handed a flyer by a young man dressed as a Harlequin. Which amused me greatly. So, I told her how I had been high on gas and suddenly found myself holding a flyer. That had tickled her! The woman is very easy to talk to. I like that in a person. The girl returns and sits in the seats behind the woman opposite me, I guess so she can have some privacy. She does not realise that I can see her reflection in the window and can see she is listening to us. Noticing… These days it is wrapped up as mindfulness. But I call it noticing. I notice things.

"I mean, I'd be fine if it turns out to be a boy," continues the woman opposite me, "but I wouldn't really know what to do with him. Like, how would I make sure he doesn't grow up to be a total arsehole, like one of them men next door…"

"I think it's the same as with any child," I reflect. "If you give them love and security, most children avoid becoming awful."

It makes me think of my sister, who hadn't been awful when we were little. She'd been an adorable little girl with blonde bouncing curls. Everyone had fallen for her. Including me. But having been bullied by my mother her whole life, with no feelings of security, it had all left her... Well... Spikey.

"The most annoying thing about doing IVF," the woman goes on, "is that it steals all the pleasure from what ought to be the fun and magical bit. The shagging and conception. That's the fun bit. If it works, that's when the real worries start. Then I'll be stressing about having a miscarriage, then about giving birth, then about protecting a vulnerable baby, then bringing them up, then them going off and becoming teenagers. It just feels shit to be robbed of the only fun bit of the whole bloody process!"

"Well you can still have sex..." I laugh, and the woman joins in.

"Yes, but it's so unromantic, having baby-making-sex. Oh my god, it's awful. We've been doing it for years now; taking my temperature, sticking my feet up in the air after every shag. Every period feeling like a little miscarriage. It's just so unsexy. I feel like all my sex appeal has disappeared. When we realised we had to do IVF, we got this cardboard box through the post full of injections and my husband was like, 'Yay, we're gonna make a science baby!' and if it works out then that will be the start of my child's life and I'm totally neurotic and strung out now. I don't want to be all precious over my baby and suffocate it. I'm scared that's what I'm going to do. It's just horrible."

"That doesn't sound like fun…" I muse.

"No… Listen, thank you for asking me about it. Honestly, I'm glad to be able to talk to someone. I can't really talk to my husband. He feels guilty as hell about what I'm having to put my body through, and my friends with babies are being unbelievably thoughtless, completely unintentionally of course, but it's excruciating. I have more in common with my trans female friends then I do with my friends who are biological mothers. Because my trans female friends advise me on what's happening to my body, with all these synthetic hormones I'm pumping into it. They sympathise with what it's like to be going through a horrific medical ordeal to try and gain something nature has cruelly refused to give me. None of my mum friends think about how hurtful it is for me to be confronted with photos of their perfect little children every freakin' day on social media… Oh dear," she catches herself ranting. "I think I'm a bit squiffy. I've not drunk booze in nearly a year!"

We both laugh and I pass her the glass of wine again and quote her my favourite saying…

"Comparison is the thief of joy."

She looks at me quizzically for a moment, then takes a sip of the wine and nods as she unpicks the sentence. I crunch my way through a few nuts and look at the side of the girl's face in the reflection. She looks as if she's had a hard life.

"Most people just force advice on me," continues the woman across from me. "For some reason my reproductive organs seem to be public property these days. Anyone can talk about them. You know nearly everyone I speak to asks me who the problem is. As in which one of us is infertile, me or my husband. How outrageous is that!? It's like they don't seem to realise they're basically asking, *Does your husband's cock not work or is it your fanny that's busted?* I mean, no one ever asks strangers questions like that normally, but if you're a woman doing IVF, it's basically fair game…"

This makes her snort at herself.

"And if anyone," she continues, "tells me one more time they know a couple who got pregnant as soon as they stopped trying, then I swear to god I'm going to fucking kill them. Sorry… Excuse my language."

"I don't mind" I laugh.

"*Just relax* they say," she clearly is getting quite drunk now, *but she bloody well deserves it,* I think… "Well we've been trying for six years. We haven't been stressing out every time we've had fucking sex over the last six years for fuck sake. And plenty of stressed people get pregnant all the time. It's literally got nothing to do with it. It's just so inappropriate to be telling people all they need to do is relax."

She hands the wine back to me again.

"I think I owe you an apology then," I reflect. "As I think that's pretty much what I just said to you earlier..."

"Oh no," The woman leaps to life, feeling guilty, "I didn't mean to suggest..."

"No, don't worry. Thinking about it, I'm probably guilty of having done that many times. And the couple I know did happily fall pregnant after they stop trying IVF. About three years after. And I've definitely told woman trying for kids that story before..."

"That's fine, I understand why it might seem useful to share these anecdotes. People just want to help. But there are also thousands of couples that never get pregnant, regardless of whether they 'stopped trying' or not. No one ever tells you about them though. Or how they coped with the heartache. What are their lives like now? There are no role models in this world for barrenness. Expect for, like, Tom Thumb. Or something."

"I know lots of positive stories about women who don't have children," I muse, changing tact slightly. "Me being one of them."

"You don't have any children?" asks the woman.

"Nope. I never wanted them. And I have a fabulous life…" I toast myself with the wine.

"You just knew you didn't want them?" she quizzes me.

"Yep." I respond. "My mother told me and my sister, almost daily, that we should never have children. She drummed it into us. And there was never a moment when it even crossed my mind."

I pour more wine into the glass.

"Not everyone should have kids. Why is it we think that everyone has a god given right to have children? I mean, not everyone should be teachers. Many people in this world should not be allowed to be responsible for the life of another person. My mother being one of them. She should have never been allowed to have children."

"Tell me about it," the woman responds. "Try sitting on a bus when you're doing IVF and listening to mothers swearing blue murder at their children. You spend half the day thinking, *why do they get to have kids and not me?*"

"Yes, that must be hard," I agree.

"And it's tricky, isn't it?" she muses, "I didn't want kids when I was in my twenties. I was adamant I didn't want them, but then I met my husband and suddenly I did. My body clock started ticking and it's been impossible for me to ignore it ever since. I used to even be against IVF when it first came about. Thought it was men playing Mother Nature and that it would screw up our evolution. We certainly don't need more people in the world… All that. But here I am injecting my belly every day. You can't tell people they can't have kids. It's too big a primal urge. Like telling people they can't have sex. They'll find a way around it. You'll just push everything underground."

∞

Meh, I think, shifting in the seat behind them. What that old woman just said was spot on… Kind of blew my mind. What a great idea… Parents being vetted before they're allowed to have kids; sounds like a great idea to me. Like going for a job interview or something. What a fucking awesome idea. The world would be such a better place for it…

∞

I look out the window and notice a fox looking up at the train with interest.

"Oh, hello friend!" I start, and the woman I've been chatting to sits up and peers out, seeing him too. Then I clock that the younger woman also looks and so clearly is still listening to us.

The banks of the track slope down to the flood plain fields on either side and are lined with ivy, freshly leaved ash trees and wildflowers of mugwort and red valerian. The fox is a big one and healthy looking. He's a real beauty. He catches sight of the three of us staring at him and gives a little start, which makes us all snigger with delight. But after a moment he realises he's safe and saunters off, tail hung heavy and low, as he weaves between the undergrowth, disappearing into a ditch. Two fat and startled wood pigeons tumble inelegantly from the boughs above him and fly off to safer climes.

We sit and enjoy the view for a while. The sky now lightly washed with a few remaining hues of pink, as the blue begins tumbling in to engulf us.

"Have you heard of John O'Donohue?" I ask, and the blonde lady opposite me shakes her head. "Well then you're in for a treat. I read his works on rotation. Him… T. S. Elliott and Julian of Norwich. Look at this…"

∞

The woman, clearly pleased to share her treasure, digs out a gorgeous white, gold and battered well-loved book, entitled *Divine Beauty*. She opens it and begins to read:

"Our time is hungry in spirit. In some unnoticed way we have managed to inflict severe surgery on ourselves. We have separated soul from experience, become utterly taken up with the outside world and allowed the interior life to shrink. Like a stream that disappears underground, there remains on the surface only the slightest trickle. When we devote no time to the inner life, we lose the habit of soul. We become accustomed to keeping things at surface level. The deeper questions about who we are and what we are here for visit us less and less. If we allow time for soul, we will come to sense its dark and luminous depth. If we fail to acquaint ourselves with soul, we will remain strangers in our own lives."

"Gosh." I respond, unable to even begin to express how much that resonates with me. I don't even know where to start. I see the hunger she's just described in everything. In everyone. Alcoholism, suicide, depression. It's everywhere I look. And not just in strangers, but in close friends and family. Even in myself.

We sit in a comfortable silence absorbing the words. I study the trees that line the tracks and suddenly think to myself how I have no idea of their names. I know oaks, weeping willows, silver birches and… Yep, I think that's about it. The rest I can't differentiate. I have no idea what the tree beside me is, though I know I like it. I call it a fractal tree in my head, because when I used to lay around in fields, off my face on drugs, a lifetime ago it feels like now, these were the ones I liked looking up through best. They're kind of like a *Magic Eye* image…

I begin to grow uncomfortable with the silence. Even though I'm trying to play it cool in front of this awesome woman, I'm in awe of her and find myself desperate to make her think I'm as cool as she is.

"There's childless and childfree isn't there?" I suddenly come up with, picking up a thread of our previous conversation.

"I don't know," she responds, "what's the difference?"

"Childfree," I explain, proud to know something that she doesn't, "is when you don't *want* kids. Childless is when you want kids, but you can't have them. I'm childless, and you are childfree."

"I've never heard of those terms before," the older woman replies, turning and facing me again with those flaming orange eyes. "But hopefully, you'll only be childless for the moment," and she smiles at me, encouragingly.

I smile back at her and sigh. A deep sigh of sadness. I feel it roll up, right from within the depths of my womb.

"And if it doesn't work out," suggests the older woman tentatively, "then perhaps your next job is to see if you can find a way back to feeling childfree again. If you once felt childfree, then perhaps there's the possibility of doing a pond dip back down into your soul and navigating your way home to a place where you can live happily in a world without having any children. Perhaps you might be able to feel…" she couldn't quite think of the word, but came up with "powerful, about your situation. It's not a powerful choice, because it's not a choice, but you may be able to find a way to powerfully accept the situation."

I think about it... I don't really like to imagine the IVF not working. But it's a distinct possibility. Each go only has a 50/50 chance of success after all. A deep hot fear, that seems to have become a constant friend of mine, creeps up from my womb and sweeps over my body. It's a longing so acute it tastes of metal. But through the searing heat of the stomach-wrenching pain, I sense a golden honey like light piercing through the darkness, as I imagine myself in a future where I'm okay with being childless. Accepting it to the point where I could happily call myself childfree. I imagine this version of myself, travelling the world, sleeping in every morning, feeling smug about helping to save the planet and not having to worry about a future that I suspect is going to be fucking horrendous. This version of myself looks like she's living a wonderful life. Trying on this possibility for size, the image soothes my soul.

"I guess so..." I respond

MOTHER

Hi Mother Earth

Hello sweetheart, how in the cosmos are you?

I'm great, thanks mum. Just wondered if I could ask you a few questions?

Of course, my darling. I'm a multitude of ears…

Well… In the archetypal realm, do you feel that there is a mobilisation amongst the feminine archetypes? Is a paradigm shift occurring?

Well, there's always a paradigm shift occurring darling; it's why I never get bored. If you think of it like a kaleidoscope, tiny little shards of reality are forever moving. What seems small and inconsequential at first, after a few twists of the wheel, suddenly reveal a whole new image that's completely different; yet still made up of the same components. It never ceases to amaze me what comes up.

Are you despondent or tired of humanity?

I'm the original mother and no matter how awful humanity treats me you'll always be my little fluffy bottoms… I still love you, no matter what, and hope that one day you'll stop taking me for granted and realise we could be such friends. I look forward to sitting and watching the sunsets with you again.

Can you forgive us?

You're my children and I love you. There's nothing to forgive! I just want to be part of your lives again.

Can we come back from here then?

Yes. But look; the sooner the better, because you're all becoming addicts my love. And you know you are. The further down this road you go the harder it is going to be to come back. Nothing is ruined yet, you're still young, but if you don't do something pretty damn sharpish, you're in danger of utterly ruining your life. And all life… I hate to be a spoil sport, but it's true. You need to make the choice to change things and then put the work in to make it happen. It's not going to be easy. Nothing good ever comes from easy.

What do I need to do?

Stop thinking about yourself the whole time; that would be a good start, and start thinking about *how you can be of service to others... I mean, what is your contribution to the world? Stop waiting to be discovered and get on with it. You see, it's not all about you. You are a unique being who has been given your own special musical note. But it doesn't make <u>you</u> special. Everyone has a unique note. Your job is to learn to sing your note loud and clear, then be of service to the symphony in its entirety. You are all in this together and without each other you're nothing more than an E-flat. What are you bringing to the table sweetie and how can you live it as fully as possible? By all means, sing your note and sing it loud! But also listen.*

And take care of your health. Eat well. Keep your home tidy and clean. Don't be late. Get plenty of exercise; that kind of thing. Don't spend all day in front of a screen. Go for lots of walks and get outside whenever possible. Listen to the birds. Learn the names of all the trees. Notice when spring begins. Take time to sit and breathe and do nothing. Don't work all the time. Go on holiday. Follow your passions. Fall in love, hopelessly, again and again and again. Never become bitter. Don't blame others. Love yourself and everyone around you. See your brothers and sisters through my eyes. I love you. I love all of you. And I made you all, so of course you're all utterly fabulous.

How's Dad?

He's tired, I think. I haven't seen him in a very long time.

Does he feel any love or compassion towards you still?

Of course he does, he can't live without me. Deep down I know he misses me, but he had a point to prove, that he could do better than me and that he didn't need me. And for a long time, he was right. But now he's forgotten how to express himself without shouting and he's shouted himself hoarse, and he is run down and worn out. He's destroyed everything he loves in the name of power and he's either going to obliterate himself or he's going to have a nervous breakdown. Either way he's going to have to chill out and remember who he really is. He certainly can't go on like this for much longer.

Would you ever take him back?

Oh sweetheart… Our dance is as old as time and we are one thing experiencing each other subjectively as separate entities, but we are not separate. Like you and all your brothers and sisters. We are sharing the same infinity. It's a tango… And there is no tango without a tango partner. He's in me and I'm in him. Quite literally sometimes.

That's gross.

Oh, don't be such a prude.

Have you anything else you want to say to me before I go?

Yes. I do… I have all the love in the world for you, my child, but you are not my first and you will not be my last. Your time here is short, so make the most of it… What legacy do you want to leave behind? How do you want to be remembered? You're 21 now… It is the 21st Century. You're a grown up. Who are you going to be in the world? Now get on with it and clear this bloody mess up because you're a grown up now and I'm not going to do it for you. And if you don't clean it all up quick smart then I'll be forced to throw you out and you'll soon discover you have nowhere else to go.

And stop being so uptight… Take more mushrooms for the heaven's sake.

NIGHT

"Well," Alice piped up, "be they mother or son, they hath both forsaken me. I prayed to them both. And I prayed, and I prayed, and I prayed…"

"But did thou pray for thy will or God's will?" asked the cunning woman.

"I prayed for a child…" she went on, "and they would have been a child of God. I see not why I should be punished for yearning with all my heart, for what any good wife wants!"

"Thou art not being punished for what thou were yearning for," insisted Marjorie, "Thou art being punished, by men, for what thou were going to do about it. Casting spells at Beltane... It is for that you will swing."

"It was not a spell, it was a prayer," retorted Alice, her humours rising.

"And in truth," Marjorie went on, "Mayhap it was not our good Lord or Mother Mary's will…"

"Thou old witch!" spat Alice, going for the old woman, with her claws outstretched.

The young girl, who was still sat between them, held Alice back and Marjorie stepped up and out the way, feigning that the goblet was dry and needed refilling. Alice was furious that Marjorie showed no signs of remorse, and just made her way over to the cabinet, taking out another bottle of the communal wine.

Turning back to Alice, she then retorted;

"Mistress… If I be one, then thou art one too."

And she was right, Alice realised, as rocks filled her heart…

For all, she thought, *shall say that me being at the tree with the cunning woman on Beltane is witchcraft to be sure and that I was casting spells. All them meddling gossips will care not how my heart is filled with pain and I have tried all else to bring on a babe. Every old wives' recipe and all the never-ending advice. I have tried all the priests hath bid me. I have prayed in all ways - of the old and the new faiths. I have prayed on my knees in the church and by my bed at night for a score or more years and I have prayed in screams at the wind on top of Winelton Hill so that God might hear me better. But he hath not heard me. He hath only forsaken me. So yes, I did then pray to the yew tree. But it were not witchcraft, it were my last hope. And now I am utterly hopeless…*

∞

That shut up the foolish scowl, thought Marjorie with satisfaction.

They all fell into a silence.

How dare she call me a witch, Marjorie began to brood, *and her here with the same fate as me. And her "prayer" in my basket. How dare she!*

She'd returned to the bench and they sat in silence and plotted a hundred curses upon each other.

The light was dimming fast. The sky now emptied of pink hues and quickly deepening into darker and darker blues. They sat and stared into the growing blackness of the church, as the shadows lengthened. Creeping fingers of pious outstretched hands, cast by the statues of Saints, reached out towards them across the stone flanked floor, with promises of loving kindness; but their smashed off faces no longer shared their mercy.

∞

Kitty began to realise that she feared spending the night in this drafty church. She had not thought it would come to this; that her father would leave her here, in such a situation. But with each passing moment, the truth of it set in, like creeping black water that could not be held back. *We will face this trial,* she thought to herself, *if we are lucky then we will receive a fair hearing. If we are unlucky… We will be tortured until we confess. Our fates lie completely in the hands of men. Some are men who are meant to love us, so hopefully they do. I think, I hope, my father loves me… I hope the plump one's husband loves her too. I do not know who there is to love the old woman though.* Kitty thought back to the fellow who had kicked the plump one as they had been dragged into the church. He had seemed most aggrieved with the cunning woman. Kitty wondered what that might have been about. Many of the villagers, Kitty mused, were suspicious of her already. She being so old and a widow… Or a spinster mayhap? Kitty knew not what. Rumours ran about the parish that she was a witch and others said that she had arrived in Winelton completely destitute and a vagabond, many summers past. Though this confused Kitty as the old woman spoke with a fair tongue, as if she once had been a gentlewoman. Not like the plump one. One thing Kitty knew for sure about the old Mistress, was that the woman had no family.

Kitty looked through the darkening room at the two women on the bench. She knew nothing about the plump one or why her fellow had not come for her. *Mayhap she had been a shrew to him,* she wondered. *Her temper doth suggest she might well have been. Mayhap he will be pleased to be rid of her?* Kitty's thoughts fell to her own father. *Mayhap he felt the same of me,* she considered. *Am I not also a shrew? And an embarrassment? Then what of the priest… Would it not be well for him to be rid of me?*

"In truth, could it really be that the three of us will swing upon the morrow?" Kitty whispered with despair into the darkness.

Her words were met with silence.

∞

"What thinketh thou they will they do to us upon the morrow?" spluttered Alice suddenly, turning in desperation, "when they come for us? Will they beat us and poke us with devil's sticks? Will they?"

"Oh, stop thinking on it!" shouted the cunning woman. "Doth thou think it will be any better if we keep going over and over it? Thou wilt not die one death, but wilt die fifty." She turned and looked at Alice, holding her desperate gaze, "think on the hazelnut. Think on pulling out of this world. Think on what is on that hazelnut. <u>Everything</u> is on that hazelnut."

Alice sat and thought on this for a time.

"Well, for this I will need more wine," she huffed, and Marjorie passed her the goblet with a little chuckle. Alice felt a little forgiven.

∞

"Shall I see thee both again?" Kitty whispered, "upon the other side?"

"Of course, thou wilt," laughed the old woman, rubbing Kitty's thigh vigorously, "thou shall not be rid of us…"

"Wilt we not all go to hell?" brooded the plump one.

"Ha!" snorted the old woman, shocking the other two, "it will be them bloody men and that priest who will all go to hell."

They fell back into a shocked silence.

The birds outside were singing their evening chorus. A blackbird was visible in silhouette on the yew tree and its song echoed around the vaulted ceiling. Kitty suddenly felt awfully hungry. She had not eaten since breaking her fast. She had been chaperoned with her sisters down to the green by Joan and her Governor, Master Jack, after they had all re-grouped at the house once the service had finished. Their father had greeted them at the green and showed them where they should be seated; all sat together at the high board, along with the Goodwin's, whom her father was gratuitously grovelling over. Montague had been there, and Kitty had been expected to sit beside him...

But the hog had not finished roasting; there had been problems with the fire, according to her father, who was waxing lyrical about the idleness of common folk, and so Kitty did not yet have to take her place at the board, and had no intention of sitting down unless she had to. She asked Joan if she would take a turn with her about the green. Joan, who was happily in conversation with one of the Earl Goodwin's stewards, made no attempt to conceal her grievance at being taken away from the table, but she did as Kitty asked, and they circled the festivities. A company of mummers players performed *George and the Dragon* in the centre of the green, which celebrated the death and rebirth cycle of the year and had always been performed, every spring, since time began, Kitty thought. It told the story of a quack doctor pouring the elixir of life into the mouth of a dead St George, after he had fought and died at the hands of the Saracen Knight. He was then resurrected with an incantation: "Elecampane! Elecampane! It brings the dead to life again!" St George would always be brought back to life and all the crowd would always cheer. Kitty had seen the play every spring for all her twenty springs, but it never failed to please her and never was it performed the same way twice. It was a delight to see each year how it would be changed. The priest had been sermonising earlier on how plays were sinful and papist, so she had wondered if it would be allowed to happen again next year. Now she thought on how she would never find out. And then the maypole dancing had begun, and Joan had been grabbed by the same steward to dance. Kitty had let her go and used the opportunity to make her escape. That was when she had made her way back up the lane to the churchyard, knowing that everyone else was safely back at the green.

Kitty's stomach rumbled loudly.

The plump one reached into her hanging pocket and pulled out two biscots. She broke them into pieces and handed a piece to Kitty and one to the other woman. They sat and ate them in silence for a time, staring up and out at the fading blue light behind the great window.

"So, what's thy story then?" asked the cunning woman suddenly, pulling Kitty back from her thoughts, "what was thou doing wandering about the village with a curse in thy bodice, out of thy father's library?"

"My stepmother left me with many sisters," Kitty sighed, "and Father wants me bred and married."

"Who would he have thee marry?" asked the old woman.

She could hardly bring herself to say his name… "Montague Crete…" she replied.

The other two women almost wretched in distress at the news, faces wracked with disgust.

"Most recently," Kitty went on, perturbed by their reaction, "there be only so many times he will let me say nay, and I be not getting any younger."

∞

It filled Marjorie with fury, for her to think of this fair maid in the hands of that… Cretin. "Your father would not wish thee upon that vile beast?"

"My father has no sons and what other purpose may I and my sisters fulfil?" the girl asked.

"But his temper!" Alice shrieked.

Montague Crete was famous about the Parish for his foul moods and acts of violence against the commoners who had the misfortune of catching his attention. He was known for beating his house staff and gossip was that he had beaten his squire to death, though a horse was blamed for trampling him. Crete was ugly and repulsive in equal measure, both on the outside and within.

"And his breath" Alice went on. "Eurgh… I would not let him lay a finger on me."

"He touched me once…" Marjorie confessed. Montague Crete had once stumbled upon her on his way home from the tavern, heading back to his grand house at the other end of the village. She had been returning from delivering a baby and was covered in blood. Something about the sight of her, all bloody and dishevelled under the full moon, had aroused him and he had tried to bustle her into the Blacksmith's forge, pulling at her skirts and slobbering all over her face and neck. She'd grabbed his bollocks hard with her hand and twisted them. He'd screamed and went to strike her, but the Blacksmith, Master Peter, had been in the shadows napping. Hearing the commotion, he'd roused saying "Aye, Aye, what's going on here then?" Montague had jumped out of his skin and Marjorie made her escape, leaving the two men quarrelling behind her.

Marjorie looked up and saw the other two women were horrified, "It was but once," she soothed them.

"It would be better to be hung, then pawed by him," Alice swallowed.

"That be a thing to think on," jeered Marjorie, "that will cheer thee up as thy little feet begin to dance. Montague Crete and his big fat leery face."

"Mayhap thou should shout that out at the gallows," suggested Alice. *"I'd rather swing then be touched by thee!"*

"Better the ropes kiss!" shouted the girl.

The cunning woman smiled at both their spirits. "They canst take that away from thee, can they?" she reassured them. "They might choke thy little throat out, but they can't stop what comes out of it. I shall say my Hail Marys, right at the priest. And what then can they do to me then? They think they're hanging me for being cunning. Little do they know they've got a Catholic on their hands! Mayhap they'll cut me down and burn me when they find out. Look at this, look..."

Excitedly, she began to pull up her skirts, but they were not skirts that should be pulled up. They were mucky and smelt as if they had never been removed, let alone washed, which they had not. Both the younger women recoiled as the foul air hit their noses, but then Alice spotted what she was trying to show them and gasped. Embroidered in red silk thread, standing out in stark contrast to the yellow linen of the petticoat, was a crucifix. The banned icon of the old faith.

Marjorie continued, "this hath been on my person these last ten summers. They never think to look here."

"But they will see it upon the morrow!" blurted Alice, full of terror. "Thou should take it off and hide it in the church somewhere."

"Well I could cover it with thy prayer; for the yew tree," she mocked. "And they can hang me twice and then burn me for being papist."

"Thou could take my curse too and be hung three times." suggested the girl, laughing nervously.

"They can hang me three times for a curse found in a library!" Marjorie laughed.

They all laughed at this, a little drunkenly, then all three went quiet and contemplated the truth of it. Marjorie began to whisper her Hail Marys, making Alice look up to the rafters of the church, as if she were checking to see if God would punish them with a bolt of lightning.

∞

For a long time, the old woman whispered her prayers and they sat; transfixed by her ceaseless chanting. The sky outside was now a dark blue; just about to turn black. The yew tree could only just be picked out against it as a shadow. The temperature suddenly dropped, and the plump one began to drag her sleeves around from the back of her bodice, where they have been tucked into the strings of her apron. She tugged them loose and pulled up and over her arms.

They could hear owls calling to each other from the other side of the window, highlighting the vastness of the space beyond the church; making their confines ever more encroaching. Kitty's bodice was beginning to cut into her armpits and her head ached from the tightness of her hair. She had never intended to keep it up for this long.

Seeing that the plump woman was making

herself more comfortable, Kitty decided to let her hair down. She could make it neat again before the morn. Taking off her pearl trimmed black boxed bonnet, which sat on her head like the point of a diamond, she set about pulling out each of the pins that had kept it in place and carefully stowed these in the layers of her bodice. She placed her bonnet gently beside the altar and removed her white lace edged coif and placed this beside the bonnet too. Untying the braid that held her two plaits in place above her head, she let them fall and set about untangling the hair until it tumbled loose about her shoulders in wavy locks.

She noticed how the two women looked upon her now. Compared to them she was fair and in the prime of her youth; with perfect white skin and long hair of spun gold. But she did not care for her pretty face or fine flowing hair. All Kitty wanted was to be free and that meant being something other than a kept maid and merchant's daughter. If she had been poor, like the rest of the village girls, she would have at least grown up with friends and could have married whomever she pleased. But as a merchant's daughter she had no choice but to marry whomever her father set her to marry, and that choice would be made for political gain, not for love nor comfort. Not that there was anyone in the village she could love. Many men looked upon her hungrily, but the thought of all of them repulsed her. Sometimes though, when she looked upon Joan, or when Joan helped her to bathe, thoughts had crossed her mind…

∞

Suddenly Alice heard the noise of the festivities coming from down at the green, carried up the path by a change of wind, and a lump came to her throat. She could not stop herself from thinking on how John would be there now with Marigold, drunk and knowing he would soon be a widower and able to have his fill. She looked over at the large wooden door, now crouching ominously in the darkness.

"The sun is down," said the young girl, breaking the desperate silence.

"Might we light a candle yet?" asked Alice, sickened suddenly by the night, which had come upon them, removing all hope that the evening's events had been a foolish mistake.

"Nay, not yet," whispered Marjorie, "let us enjoy the last light from the sky."

They all looked up at the large window and watched the light ebb away as the stillness of night began to take hold.

"A bat is out," noticed Marjorie.

"And the first star," whispered the maid.

For a long time, they sat in silence and watched the star twinkling.

"What if my sister is to marry him now instead?" asked the young woman's voice from the darkness, her fair skin and shoulders now only just visible in the gloom beneath the window.

Alice felt the tension between herself and Marjorie, all filled with knowing. Daughters were like horses. If one was lame, then it meant nothing for the rider, as long as there be another for him to ride instead.

"Here," says Marjorie, thinking on distraction, "this be the perfect charm for Montague Crete. Doth thou know what this be?" she asked, as she began to rifle around in her basket, before pulling out a piece of cheese cloth, which she unwrapped.

An ungodly smell filled the church, coming from the contents; like a dog's fart or rotten meat. The other women recoiled as the stench hit them.

"What is it?" gasped the young maid.

"It's what a fellow keeps in his codpiece," boasted Marjorie.

"What!" Alice gulped, thinking that Marjorie had in truth cut off a fellow's cod.

Laughing at her reaction, Marjorie explained "this be a barbed cod."

"Tis it a pig's?" asked the young woman.

"Nay," laughed Marjorie. Everyone knew a pig's cod is corkscrew, "tis a fox's cod. Now, in order that thy sister doth not get settled with that old Montague, there will be some cunning we can do with this."

"Ooo…" Alice cooed, suddenly liking the idea that they still had a little power left at their disposal, "could she take it forth to the gallows with her and shout a curse at Montague, that his own cod will shrivel up like this one?"

"How will I get it to the gallows with me?" asked the young woman.

"I'm sure there be some place we can hide it." Alice considered, beginning to fiddle with the girl's long hair.

"Well," said the cunning woman; making her way over to the young maid and waving the rancid penis in the air suggestively. The maid began to rise nervously, knowing something in the woman's tenor meant she was about to do something to her. A strange thought crossed Alice's mind, that this be one of the most exciting moments of her life...

"Now that thou doth mention it," smirked Marjorie, with a sly smile, "thou hath just bought to mind that there be one place you could hide it…" and she went for the girl and tried to pull up her skirts. The girl shrieked and leapt back laughing. Alice laughed too. She had never laughed liked this before.

Someone banged hard on the door.

"What's going on in there?"

Shouted a voice.

The girl dropped down to the floor and they all fell silent. Alice thought that she had known that voice… *Was that, Pip the Bake house boy?* She thought. *If that was Pip, then*

John knew for sure that I am here... He is not coming for me...

No more sounds came.

Marjorie began to laugh again quietly in the darkness. Then the girl whispered;

"I'd rather hang!"

Marjorie started to crawl in the darkness towards the altar, making the girl squeal as she tried desperately to make her escape. Marjorie whispered in nursey rhyme tones;

"Oh Montague Crete, who lives on the street, he's viler than all be far. His breath is a furnace. His feet are far worse..."

"And no one would like him if it weren't for his purse!" Alice joined in, feeling utterly proud of the swiftness of her wit.

They all laughed together quietly.

"Now that's what I will shout at them as they lead me up to the gallows. I'll sing that song and then I will curse them all."

In the darkness her words sounded terrible.

"Well I will say my Hail Marys," whispered Marjorie. "Right at the priest."

“I doth not know the Hail Mary,” admitted the maid.

“What?” Alice shrieked in disbelief.

“She is too young,” Marjorie pointed out. “It starts…”

And in the blackening room the old woman taught the young maid the Lord’s Prayer. It sounded powerful, being whispered in the darkness, and Alice realised how much she has missed it and began to join in; finding comfort in the old familiar words.

“Holy Mary Mother of God. Pray for us sinners now and at the hour of our death,” whispered Marjorie.

“Holy Mary Mother of God. Pray for us sinners now and at the hour of our death,” repeated the girl, and Alice followed…

“Amen” finished Marjorie.

“Amen” they whispered.

“There…” asked Marjorie “Doth that not make thee feel better?”

“Aye,” agreed the maid, “though mayhap that be the wine.”

Marjorie laughed and threw the smelly cheese cloth at the girl, which had been wrapped around the old fox penis, making the girl squeal and leap out of the way.

They all put their fingers to their lips and looked at the door expectantly, but no one stirred the other side. Alice looked to see where the fox penis had gone and snorted as she saw that Marjorie had wickedly left it sitting in the middle of the altar.

Stopping and thinking for a moment, Marjorie asked the girl, "When thou wrote thy curse in the library, what did you hope it would do?"

The girl thought on this for some time. Then she looked up at them both and whispered; "I hoped it would help me to escape…"

∞

I'm feeling quite merry. We've drunk the wine and are now making a start on the ale. Juliette, which is the older woman's name, tried again earlier to offer some wine to the young girl sitting behind us, before it ran out, but she turned it down. But she did eventually accept some water a little later and then sat back down in the seats across from us, which feels less weird.

"Do you think we could climb out the train and walk back to Beswick?" asks Juliette. The driver recently announced that there have been more obstacles found along the tracks, so the train is now stuck in both directions. The police have been called and engineers are clearing the tree, but we're still stranded for the foreseeable.

Trying to peer down the side of the tracks we both draw the same conclusion… "It's too steep isn't it?" I suggest.

"Yes, I think you're right." Juliette agrees.

"Do you think it might be a terrorist attack?" I ponder out loud.

"HA!" Juliette blurts out loudly, making me jump slightly. "Bloody terrorist attack… Why would anyone want to tamper with an almost empty train in the middle of rural Sussex?"

"I guess so…" I respond, feeling a little stupid.

"It will just be some high-spirited lads entertaining themselves on a Saturday night," Juliette went on.

I feel even less like walking along the tracks, if it means we might happen across some 'high-spirited' youths, in the middle of nowhere.

The door to our carriage swooshes open and I turn around to see a man with a shaved head stagger in. He's surprised to see us and shouts back over his shoulder,

"Oi! Did you know there's a bunch of birds back here?"

Two other men appear behind him and look at us. Their faces clearly drop when they see we're not exactly their type.

"Yeah, they're all fucking dogs!" shouts the awful man who'd harassed us earlier. The men checking us out laugh and walk back into the other carriage.

"That's never stopped you," we hear them laughing at him.

The door swooshes closed again, leaving the shaved headed man alone with us. He smiles at us provocatively and walks into the toilet.

He begins to piss without bothering to shut the door.

"Charming," tuts Juliette.

As he comes back out, I make the mistake of turning around again. Doing up his flies, he pauses and winks at me, "don't worry sweetheart, I'll be back."

I snort in disgust and turn away, as Juliette shouts over my shoulder,

"Did you remember to flush?"

He grunts and leaves. We all sit in silence for a moment. I strain, listening to the men, making sure he's gone, and that their attention has moved elsewhere.

"I mean," Juliette starts up, "what is a virgin, mother or hag these days?" We had been in the middle of this conversation before the driver's announcement. "I'm not a virgin, mother or hag. YOU'RE not a virgin, mother or hag. I'm guessing she's not a virgin, mother or hag," she adds flippantly, pointing her beer at the young girl.

I force back a smile. The poor young woman clearly doesn't want to get dragged into any of this.

"... therefore, we need new archetypes," she insists.

"Yes," I agree. "I mean how long are we meant to be crones for these days anyway, seeing as we're living so much longer? Are we expected to be crones for half our lives?"

"Exactly!" laughs Juliette. "I've got another thirty, maybe forty years in me, hopefully, and I'll have been a crone for all that time. If I live to 96 then I'll have been one for half my life! It all needs a rethink."

"We need to rethink our stockpile of polite conversation questions too. You know, ones like *do you have children?* And *would you like to have children?* Because when we ask those stupid questions, we don't even really care about the answers, but we're inadvertently causing people genuine pain. I mean, how often do people ask things like *who was the last person to die that you loved?"*

"Tom," answered Juliette.

"What?" I say, laughing.

"Tom passed away four years ago this summer," she explains.

"Oh gosh, I'm so sorry," I try to back track, realising the woman is serious.

"Don't worry, I like to talk about him. I wish people did ask me about him more often actually, because everyone just tip toes around the subject and it means I don't really get to talk about him anymore and celebrate all the wonderful things he was and still is to me."

"I can't even begin to imagine what it would be like to lose my husband." I reflect, having never really wanted to think on such thoughts. "Does it get easier with time?"

"No" Juliette responds. "It gets harder. The longer the amount of time that passes, the more real it becomes that he won't be coming back."

"I'm so sorry," I stammer.

"Don't be... You've done nothing wrong," she responds, warmly.

We look out the window in slight awkwardness. I don't really know what to say to her now. Nothing I say will make it better.

The sky has turned dark blue and the clouds hang in black drapes across the sky.

"I keep thinking about committing suicide." I blurt out. I don't even know why I just decided to say that, of all the things! Other than the fact I can't think of anything else to talk about and I instantly feel stupid, as if I've tried to trump her story or something. I feel like a complete idiot.

"Why? Aren't you surrounded by people who love you?" she asks me.

I feel revolting… "Yes. Utterly."

She looks at me, down her nose, with a serious, almost stern face.

"How you are feeling is real, don't doubt it. I can see it in you. But if you do kill yourself, you will rip layers of pain into the hearts of the people who love you in ways you cannot possibly imagine. And I know you can't imagine, because if you could, you would not be considering this as an option. And the ones you love are not just your family and close friends, but anyone and everyone whom you have ever known. People you might not have seen in years will also be left feeling bereft. And that's the only word for it. Bereft. Like you're a bomb that detonates in the centre of your world. Those closest to you will be burnt the worst, but even those on the outskirts of your life feel the blast. Every single person you have ever known will be affected by it. You must consider that... But I know when you are in this darkness, it is hard to appreciate. I understand the desperation to be freed from it all. Of course I do. We all feel it. Life is awful. But it's also magnificent. And nothing, thankfully and tragically, lasts forever. This too will pass."

"I'm sorry, I feel really stupid."

I begin to well up and start shaking my head vigorously at my selfishness for saying such a thing.

"You don't need to feel stupid. You haven't done anything wrong, but you do need to get help and get real about what this means. Are your problems so great that they warrant such damage, to people you love, who love you?"

"I just feel like such a failure. I've failed at everything."

"Some of the best people on this planet are failures. Successful people are such bores. What have they got to talk about other than bragging about how well they're doing? I don't want to hear that. I want to hear truth. I want to know you've struggled and you're still here, full of medicine to share with other people about how you've managed to hold on; how you've dragged yourself over the coals and have managed to overcome it all to be here today, with me now, in this carriage, in the middle of the night. Progression, not perfection. Curiosity… Not ambition. I don't want to hear your CV or about how much you earn. Being stuck in a carriage with a successful person would be enough to drive ME to suicide."

I snort with laughter.

She digs in her bag and hands me a tissue. Tears are rolling down my cheeks and my nose is filled with snot.

"I just feel like if I was dead, then there would still be some possibility that I could have been something, someone. I just feel like the longer I'm here, the more of a mess I'm making of everything."

"You're not making a mess. You're making a life. And lives are messy. They're all messy. If someone is making it look easy, then they're lying. Or if it isn't messy for them now then it will be at some point. Never compare yourself to anyone else. Comparison is the thief of joy, remember?"

"I like that saying," I smile.

"Your life is sacred," she says to me and this makes me burst into tears. My life feels anything but sacred.

I catch my snotty blotchy face in the reflection of the window, and it makes me well up even more. I'm broken. I am a shell of the person I was before. Before all of this. Before IVF. I used to be so full of confidence. I used to be so full of hopes and dreams. I used to be attractive. Now I'm just a washed up middle-aged nobody.

∞

Woah. That got deep. I'm feeling well awkward now and not sure if it's the mushrooms, the weed, the situation, or all three. I don't like thinking about shit like this. Especially not when I'm fucked. I mean, I feel suicidal too. Like, it's a feeling that's always there. Hanging over me. And I guess it's because there's no hope. Is there? For the future. I mean, not really. I've not really got anything to look forward to, have I? And I do think about it... A lot. About ending it all. Because anyone who hangs around is going to have to deal with some heavy old mess in the years to come. It's is going to get sooooooo messy...

The mushrooms are coming over me in waves. I decided the best thing to do in this situation is to treat being here like a form of entertainment, like *this* is the play I was going to see. So I munched another mushroom just before the woman gave me some water. It had made me gag slightly and start coughing, so I said yes when she offered it to me. A wave of it is coming over me now and I'm holding back a giggling fit. If ever there was a part of a play I should not be giggling at, this is it. Please don't giggle. I can't. Don't make them look over. I can't talk right now.

∞

I know two men who've committed suicide this year. I wish they could know how much they were loved. It makes me think of Tom too. He basically committed suicide, just very slowly. His weapon of choice being the bottle. But he couldn't cope with life either.

I read the other day that suicide is the biggest killer in men under 50. And the same article went on to say the biggest killer in women under 50 is domestic violence. Says it all really doesn't it? But that's glib...

I often do think on this though. On how the men are jumping ship. Or striking out in frustration... Well the ship is sinking. And they were most definitely in the driving seat. I mean, no one else has been allowed to have a go now, have they?

∞

"What thinks thee I should do upon the morrow?" Alice asked across the darkness.

"Laugh..." suggested Marjorie, "Curse?"

"Well," Alice rallied, "I shall curse my husband then..." and with sudden fury, she shouted at the door "for thou hath not come for me!"

"Mayhap they held him back..." suggested Marjorie, trying to quieten her down.

"You know my fellow," protested Alice, "he's as strong as an ox. If he had wished to come for me, he would be here by now. Nay, he would see me swing for not giving him an heir. Over twenty years I have loved him, cared for him, tended to him and done all a good wife should…" Turning to the door again she shouted hysterically, "well I am done with thee," and then standing up and facing the heavens she screamed, "and I am done with thee!"

"Them be strong words…" Marjorie urged, crossing to her in the darkness and grabbing her by the shoulders; trying to calm her down, but Alice pulled away and stumbled back, falling down onto the bench.

"Aye," she spat, "in truth, they be strong words, but I see no work here that maketh me love him. He hath forsaken me… He forsook me long ago… And now… Now he will hath… Well only he knows what he will hath them do to me upon the morrow. But it will be a fate worse than death, this much I am sure. If this be fatherly love for his flock, then I do renounce him. As thou hast renounced thy father," she quipped, reaching out and flapping her hand towards the young one.

Looking up at the large window, she stood up again and hobbled towards the window; her arms outstretched desperately towards the blackening sky and the ancient yew tree, "I will be a child of the moon and the stars and the rain and see what they will do with me, for I like my chances better."

Turning back to the cunning woman, Alice spat, "no more talk of God's words. And no more of that bastard priest!"

Marjorie went to her and, seizing her shoulder with one hand, thrusted the goblet of wine into Alice's hand with the other, whispering;

"Well, in truth good mistress, it is whatever will get thee through the night."

∞

With a heavy sigh, Alice dropped her head forward and she sobbed. Marjorie stood in front of her, holding her shoulders in silence as the tears rolled up in forceful waves from the depths of Alice's body. Marjorie breathed deeply, trying to soothe the woman and bring her back from the edge of terror.

When suddenly, the young one began wittering in the shadows, as if the words were ripping out of her, "I could not renounce thee, our lord. He is all I may hope for. I be cursed. It is some devil thing coming over me. A few summers back it started. My father would beat it out of me but could not. It started once when I was with that priest. I tried to keep my gaze fixed to heaven, but my eyes hurt so from staring. I should have begged Christ but could not. I was too furious. In my fury I closed my eyes and still I saw Christ and the priest..."

But then the girl realised what she was saying and sucked in a deep breath, holding her tongue and looking about her wildly. The women instinctively leapt to her side, gripping her by her arms and shoulders, for it had been as if she was having a fit. Even Alice had forgotten herself and went gone to her aid. Her voice had been strange and channelling. As if it had not been the same maid's voice. She looked wildly between them,

"Keep speaking," urged Marjorie, "might as well get it out before the morrow."

She was unsure.

∞

What Kitty was about to say; it was utterly blasphemous. And what's more, as she was just speaking the words, telling the truth of it, it had all suddenly crashed in around her. As if, until then, it had been but a dark dream; a bad trick of her awful imagination. By speaking the truth, it had all became more dreadful. More vivid and real.

"Come now girl," soothed the old woman, arms around her now, "tell us what happened to thee. Be not afeard."

Kitty swallowed hard. She breathed in the strength she needed to proceed and then said…

"It was in my mouth… Moving. Christ was looking down upon me. I felt that I might throw up from the guilt and the shame and the pain and dirt and all them rotten festering feelings. In truth, it was a sensation as if my head did split open. I felt a gross substance leak from my cracked skull and run down my face and into my mouth. The priest spilled in my mouth. Jesus wept with me.

I waited in silence. The air shook about me. I span in stillness and saw what Christ looked down upon; the perfect image of a priest and a girl, frozen. Such as a kind of baptism. The priest pulled from my mouth. I returned to my body. He left, I stayed still. Waiting. Kneeling. Dripping. Then the red-hot waves buried deep in my being came over me. I saw red. Only red. And white and glowing and burning and… And… And the still silent fury took over my body.

I woke, collapsed, face first upon the stone floor. I rose. I cleansed myself. I returned to my father's house… It was not the first time, nor the last, that the priest would call upon me; but it was when the strange waves of devil fury took hold of my body at times.

Doth thou not see? It is something within me that's rotten. Who but God may I hope for?"

The old woman shook her head furiously,

"We ain't your father, or that priest, or some other man telling thee that thou art wrong in the head, 'cause of what they have done to thee."

"It is not your fault," interjected the plump one, stroking Kitty's hair back from her sweating brow. "It be that foul priest."

Kitty filled with tears and the plump woman scooped her up in her strong arms. She buried her face in the woman's neck. The feeling of being held overwhelmed her. She had not realised, until the woman wrapped her arms around her, how much she had been waiting for this moment the whole of her life. This experience, this connection, was all she had ever dreamed of. It would have had the power to take away all the pain and the horror of her memories, had it not the bittersweet edge of being the last night of her short and pitiful life.

∞

Alice held onto the girl tightly and rocked her back and forth. Her heart was breaking in two. On the one hand she wanted to rip that sinful priest in two. And on the other hand, this was all she had ever dreamed of. To be a good mother to a young woman such as this one. And instead she would have to watch her die. They clung to each other for a long time in the darkness, weeping into each other's arms.

Marjorie eventually got up and, using a tinder box from her basket, lit one of the great candles on the altar and brought it over to the bench, shedding a warm and much welcomed glow across the rocking bodies and throwing contorted dancing shadows across the recesses of the church.

"Now look here, young lady," started the old woman, slapping the young girl's thigh. "If thou could buy thy way out of this, what would thou do?"

The young girl shook herself free from Alice's arms and sat upright, blinking furiously.

"I know not?" she sniffed, wiping her face and nose dry on her cuffs.

"Think on it…" urged Marjorie. "Let's say I was to hand thee a diamond or two, and let's say you gave one to the guard, to let thee out of here, and thou crept out of the village and up over the hill. Then what would thou do?"

The girl mulled this over and concluded, "There is not much I could do; diamonds could not turn me into a man or a fox."

"Nay," agreed Marjorie, "but they could buy thee some garments."

The girl became frustrated, "thinking on this will only make it harder upon the morrow…" she whined.

"Suppose thou doth not hang upon the morrow," pushed Marjorie, "suppose thou art given money. Will thou please construct some hope for thyself. What would thou do?"

Alice saw how this might help pass some time and distract the young maid from the darkness...

"Aye," Alice joined in, "what would thou do if thou had not been born a maid and had not all these troubles before thee?"

"Be a fellow," huffed the girl miserably.

"Suppose I am of the dark arts," teased Marjorie, "for all my love of the Virgin. Suppose I could give thee a diamond. Or two. Enough to buy thyself out of here."

"I know not where I could go..." groaned the girl, exasperated.

"Well think!" insisted Marjorie, "I ran away when I were young," which was something Alice had not known and it grabbed her interest, "with less summers than thou hath now, and I knew not where I be going or what I was going to do, so I had to make a plan... And thou taketh each step at a time and thou keeps on going until thou art where thou needs to be. So, think on it… Where would thou go?"

"Tis anywhere different?" asked the young one.

"Imagine thou wert a fellow," Alice joined in again, "and thou had fellows garments, with a great big cod piece as big as a horses and thou set thy voice a little deeper and thou went out and walked along that path and just kept on going and kept on going and kept on going, until folks thought thee a fellow… What then would thou do?"

"Wouldst thou ply a trade?" suggested Marjorie, trying to help the girl along.

"I would not wish to be like my father."

"Well that's what thou would not do…" Alice sighed. It was growing cold and she was getting tired.

∞

"Tell us not what thou would not do." Marjorie went on, driving at the point. A plan had begun forming in her mind… "Tell me what thou would do!"

The girl thought on it for a moment, and then suddenly had a revelation…

"I would join a ship!" she declared.

"Ahhhh ha!" Marjorie encouraged.

"And I would cross the high seas..." she went on.

"Well..." Marjorie replied, feeling bolstered by the young woman's compliance, "Five or six days you would be in Portsmouth. There thou could buy passage."

"I have heard tell of many a mistress who did go upon the high seas," announced Alice, with her finger in the air; suddenly seeming inebriated, "who did bind their breasts and artifice to be fellows."

"I wish I thought yesterday of such things," mumbled the maid, recalling her sorry state.

"Well that be thy problem," Marjorie scolded. "Thou hath spent so much time thinking on what thy heart doth not desire instead of thinking on what thy heart doth desire... So, come now," she whacked at the girl's thigh again, "thou art going to buy thyself out of here..."

"I will buy a big hat" she proudly proclaimed.

Alice and Marjorie burst out laughing... "Thou wilt buy a big hat!" they both mocked in unison.

"And I will play dice..." the girl smiled, suddenly having fun.

"Thou shalt buy a big hat and gamble?!" exclaimed Marjorie.

"Aye" chuckled the girl, "And I shall buy big breeches with a huge cod piece as big as a... as an Ox's and I will run away to the high seas."

Now we're getting somewhere, Marjorie thought to herself...

"Now, now, now, now, now..." Marjorie repeated, getting serious, "We need a plan. Doth thou know Portsmouth?"

"Nay" conceded the maid.

"Well then," Marjorie decided, "there be an old woman. Her name is... Mother Margaret she is called. Thou doth come in on the Portsmouth Road. There be an ash and an oak. Thou turn left at the ash. Travel down the road a little and there thou shall see an inn. It looks not like an inn... It looks like a house. Bang three times. Meow like a cat and she shall let thee in."

Alice laughed incredulously and began meowing like a cat, much to the girl's amusement, until she saw Marjorie's scowl.

"Left at the ash," repeated the maid, "look for the inn, bang three times… Meow like a cat."

"Well she doth sound like a right character," continued Alice in mockery.

"She be a friend of mine," Marjorie smarted, "and I will not have thee speak ill of her. Now, when thou arrive, tell her I sent thee as my parting gift. Tell her thy plan. Thou can lodge with her. She shall put thee upstairs. Just tell her she is not to throw thee in with the rest of the girls. And she is to find thee, and thou will have the money for this, and money speaks, especially to Mother Margaret, that she is to find thee a uniform as a sailor. But thou art not to take a low job. Thou art to take a job as a sexton or a quarter master or a quarter master's assistant."

"But I have never been to sea," insisted the girl.

"A quarter master's assistant…" Marjorie pressed on in exasperation, "she doth not even know what a quarter master is. It just means that thou must do the bills. Keep the accounts. Thou hast thy letters. But because thou hast thy letters, thou art not to be taking no lowly job where thou art hauling ropes or some such."

"And go not with some fella who is giving thee the eye," Alice warned, "for if he is giving thee the eye, he doth think thee a young lad and that will be the way he likes them."

Marjorie shook her head at Alice, before adding mischievously, "or just stick his cod in thy mouth and he will know not the difference."

To which they all laughed.

"But in earnest," Alice went on, "if they think thee a maid, they will cast thee off the ship. Tis bad luck to have a maid on a ship."

Marjorie returned to pushing Kitty with her plan.

"Thou art to live with Mother until she finds thee the clothes thou need. And she shall know all the right people to introduce thee to. All the quarter masters. They be her regular customers."

"Knock three times," humours the girl.

"Knock three times," she encourages. "Meow like a cat. Tell her I sent thee. Is that understood?"

∞

"Aye," Kitty laughed, but as she looked up at the old woman, she noticed she was nodding for her to come with her to the cabinet. Kitty screwed up her forehead and rose to join her, assuming it was to help her get more wine. Looking back at the plump one, she saw she was distracted with looking at her leg, which Kitty was shocked to see had turned a dark black already; the mark running deep into her skin like a valley of death. As she turned back towards the old woman, she discovered she was holding something out towards her. Twinkling in the candlelight Kitty saw three cut diamonds, picked out against the blue velvet cloth the woman was storing them in. Kitty stared up at her, realising she had been pressing her in earnest, and as she looked back down at the diamonds the woman wrapped them back up in the cloth, and pressed them hard into the palm of Kitty's hand. She took them and pushed the tiny bundle deep into her bodice. Kitty became flooded with heat. The excitement of possibility, of taking control of her miserable situation, having control over her life. The moment felt more charged and alive than anything she had ever felt before. Everything suddenly seemed so much more... Real. And even more terrifying. But she also felt a huge wave of guilt... What would happen to the other two women?

"Now where will this ship be going?" continued the old woman, pulling out a second bottle of wine from the cabinet "West Indies, East Indies?"

"Do I choose?" Kitty asked, feeling waves of nausea.

"Where does' thou wish to go?" the old woman snapped. "Why can thou not construct a dream for thyself girl?"

"I know not!" Kitty defended, "in all my summers none have ever let me think on thoughts such as these before."

"Thou never thought on nothing but reading books and making curses for thy father. Come on... Where art thou going to go?"

Thinking seriously upon the matter she decided, "I shall go someplace hot."

"Aye?" encouraged the woman, "and where will that be? Spain? Portugal?"

"Thou cannot trust them Spanish," piped up the plump one from the bench, "Go to Portugal, it is better."

"Africa?" the old woman suddenly suggested.

"Africa? I have never thought on Africa before," Kitty grimaced.

"There be a lot of things thou have never thought on," she teased, "When thou land in Africa, what art thou to do?"

"I know not… What are my choices?"

"Think!" she shouted suddenly, "Thou art a rich master in Africa!"

"I will need a trade," Kitty flustered.

"In very truth," she agreed, "so pick one."

"Fish?"

Both women laughed…

"Can thou fish?" the old one asked.

"Thou doth not wish to fish!" advised the other, "It is a stinking job."

Kitty mulled this over for a while and then concluded,

"I could be a merchant."

"Thou could trade silk!" agreed the older one.

"Aye," joined in the other, "thou hast thy letters."

"If thou can make a curse out of a library book then I think thou can manage work as a merchant," decided the old one, "And thou could sell silks."

"And gamble," Kitty pronounced proudly.

"And thou could take a wife," suggested the plump one, with cheeky glee.

"A wife?" Kitty exclaimed in horror, the heat rising in her cheeks.

"Aye," she went on, "I think most Mistresses would be only too happy to discover their wealthy husband was in truth a maid. Just keep a besom to hand, then thou can use the handle to..."

"There," interrupted the old one, shaking her head disapprovingly at the other woman, "thou hath a plan."

Kitty tapped the place she had safely hidden the diamonds and nodded at her.

Then the plump one rose with a groan and hobbled over to a dark corner in the church. Suddenly the sound of her pissing hard against the thresh and stone echoed around the room… All three of them cackled with delight.

∞

"And then #MeToo happened." I go on, as Juliette passes me back an opened bottle of Longman's. I've stopped crying now and I'm unashamedly pissed. Absentmindedly, I begin peeling at the label, adorned with the Longman of Wilmington.

"What was the 'me too' thing?" asks Juliette, "that kind of passed me by…"

How can a whole social movement pass someone by?

"First I heard of it," I began, trying to clear my head through the alcohol, "I saw people posting #MeToo on social media, so I

Googled what was going on and found out that an actress called Alyssa Milano had tweeted it, to share the fact she'd been molested, by using the hashtag #MeToo, and she was urging women to do the same, to highlight how many women it happened to. It was a saying she'd got from a feminist activist called Tarana Burke. It went viral. When I saw this, I uploaded #MeToo, straight away, without a second's thought. But after that, I couldn't stop thinking about it. I began to think about what my #MeToo's were. I crept down into the dark recesses of my mind and began to dig out the pains I'd sucked up and buried, bringing them out into the light. And then the memories of things that had happened to me began to circle round and around in my head.

Then I saw two women I knew, women I respect, start listing their #MeToo's on Facebook. They were graphic and awful and yet I felt like a weight was being lifted from my shoulders by reading them, and I realised that I could speak out and that I wanted to; so I wrote a list. I didn't name anyone, but I did write my list, which was..." and I began to list them. On a train. To a stranger. And to someone else who is probably also listening and just pretending not to be (the battery on her phone must have run out by now)… "That I was abused at 5 years old by two neighbourhood teenagers, I was raped at a party when I was 22 by two men while other men watched and, also when I was 22, I was too weak to say no to someone I really didn't want to have sex with, so I just went along with it. That's the one I feel worst about strangely…"

"Well that's understandable," acknowledges Juliette. "Because that time you had the most control. Yet society had already groomed you into thinking you had no right to say what you really wanted."

I take a deep sip of ale from the bottle and pass it back.

"That's exactly why," she continues, "a little slap on the bottom is not okay. It might seem like harmless fun to whoever is doing it, but it's all these little things that build up to creating a culture where women have been led to believe that they don't get to choose what happens to them…"

"Exactly!" I agree. "Well, for a moment, when that movement was building, and more and more women were sharing, I felt amazing. But I was on my way up to a meeting in London, so I didn't check my phone again until after I'd finished work. At the meeting, one of the men, clearly challenged by the upswell of the #MeToo movement that morning, felt the need to mansplain what #MeToo was 'really' all about and honestly… I wanted to kill him. On the way home, I checked my phone and I had the most notifications I've ever received. I'm a total phone addict, so I got an endorphin rush from it. But then, something changed. I started to feel sick. Up until that moment, I hadn't ever felt like I'd been raped. I hadn't ever felt like a victim. But now my whole world, my whole extended community, knew that I'd been sexually abused, and probably thought that I was a weak-willed rape victim. Everyone was sad for me, I received emails and messages from people who wanted to help me, and to be there for me. Of course, it was all meant well, but I hadn't been raped in over 16 years. No one was raping me anymore. I hadn't even felt like I'd been raped at the time. I felt like I'd done something stupid. I'd got too drunk. It was only in hindsight, as an adult, that I realised what had happened to me had not been okay.

I felt full of rage. Even the guy I'd been with at the meeting that day had hit the sad face button at some point, possibly even during the time we'd spent together, and it made me feel so naked and exposed. The worse thing was, I didn't know what to do with it... Where was I meant to put my feelings now? What was I meant to do next? My body was filled with hot fury and I wanted to erupt... But I had nowhere to put my anger. I still don't..."

"Well, you can choose to not let it make you a victim," suggested Juliette "and I always find that creativity is my outlet for such things. *Put it in the play* is what I teach at drama school."

The idea soothed me a little, but it also frustrated me.

"I'd love to go next door and thump those awful men." I erupt suddenly. "But they'd just thump me back... Much harder... I suppose you're right... I have to find ways to metaphorically thump them instead then."

∞

If you don't go thump them then I happily will... I think, as I kick my feet against the seat opposite. As she told her story, all shades of rage have risen inside me, and the more I hear those men leering and shouting in the carriage next door, the more I just want to kick the shit out of them. *Who the fuck do they think they are?*

My dad's mates used to touch me up. When my parents were both too wrecked to know what their grubby little friends were up to. They'd paw at me all the time, but one time, one of them properly touched me up and told me he'd kill me, and my dad, if I ever said anything to anyone. He was twice the size of my dad and he would have snapped him in two if he'd wanted to. I think he touched my brother as well, although he never said anything either. He liked the power he had over us. Feeling more powerful than anyone smaller than him. I think he liked feeling like he had power over my dad too. Actually... I think he might have been sleeping with my mum come to think of it. I don't know... I haven't thought of him in years. I don't ever want to think of him again.

I jump up and storm down the carriage towards the toilet and look through the door to see what the creeps are up to, being careful not to catch any of their eyes. They're all still awake and have cans of lager in their hands. How have they *still* got lager? Their faces and bald heads are bright red from having stood in the sun drinking all day. I duck inside the toilet before anyone catches my eye. It's covered in piss. That fucking arsehole. I punch the side of the toilet.

∞

I cannot, of course, help but think back to that time in the Roundhouse, in the late seventies, when I was eighteen years old and working there as the spotlight girl. The technician blocked me in the control box and attempted to rape me. I'd fought him back and he'd grabbed a metal bar to strike me with and I was sure he was going to kill me. If the stage manager had not appeared, just in the nick of time, it would have been the end of me. Thanks to him showing up, and I'm sure he must have been keeping an eye on the technician, I escaped the whole ordeal physically unscathed, although of course, it had put the fear of hell into me.

It is good, I suppose, this whole 'Me Too' thing… But what's next? What's the plan?

It's all very well, and vital, to reclaim, remember and re-own traumas, but how are you going to extract your revenge? And I'm not for one moment suggesting, necessarily, acts of violence. Revenge, as they say, is a dish best served cold. Revenge can be extracted through forgiveness and finding peace. But it can also be extracted through disarming the patriarchy... I don't like to say smashing the patriarchy. There's been more than enough smashing, thank you very much... I just want to know what you're going to do with all your anger and pain. How can it be made useful and not destructive?

If you don't transfer these emotions into action, then they fester and cause their own dramas in your psyche and often too in your physical health. These dark feelings, memories, experiences... Awful though they are, and I would never wish them upon anyone, they are also fuel. And when that fuel is transferred into creative actions directed out into the world, rather than into the self, then the dark can quite literally be transformed to good.

Then I hear a bang and think that one of the men next door have started a fight, but then

I see the girl opposite has disappeared and I guess she must have banged her head or something in the toilet. I check to make sure she hasn't caught the attention of the men next door. I hope we can get away without any further harassment from them. Their drunken banter seems to be getting louder and louder.

CRONE

One thing they don't tell you about getting old, as in really, *really*, old... is that you start seeing things from the 4th dimension. If I tried telling this to young folks, they'd just think I was off my rocker. But it's true!

In the 4th dimension, humans look like worms. You can see whole lives in their entirety. Every living moment of that person's life is packed into one. Before we get old, we experience life in the 3rd dimension, so we see everythng as a slide show of the present. But as you get older, you can remember all those slides of the present in one go, so the whole chain of present moment memories become pushed together into one long worm. These wiggly 4th dimension worms start thin at one end, with a bunch of fizzing cells, and end small again at the other end; as a pile of dust.

My experience of being a priestess of the Triple Goddess (the virgin, mother and crone) is that I have always had insight into age. I always knew that the best was still yet to come and that I would be my most awesome when I entered my crone phase, because part of me had been a crone the whole time. I remember an image that some women shared with me once, many years ago now, in a play called *Enter the Dragons*. They described womanhood as a long line of cancan dancers, made up of all the different ages of a woman's life; one for each year, standing in a long line, dancing together with their arms around each other's waists. The one at the furthest end, the one who I am now; the oldest one, is always everybody's favourite. I looked forward to becoming me as far back as I can remember. To becoming who I am now.

There is a saying: *'I wish I was, what I was, when I wished I was, what I am now.'* I think for much of my early to middle life this saying was true. Too much time was focused on some dreamt up finishing line, all glittering with success. But now I'm over all that and am happy with who I am. Although I dreamt the other day that I was young again and leapt out of bed, dislocating my hip, which was bloody annoying.

When I was younger, my older wisdom already existed in me somehow. There was always an element of me, the crone, in the younger versions of myself, which meant I always relished every age I was at in an almost nostalgic way. Every day, I was the youngest and hottest I would ever be. Every stage was something to cherish, because I always had a sense of looking back at myself with hindsight. It's why I have always documented everything and kept a journal since I was eight years old; archiving everything I have ever done. My journaling has always felt like I was writing down a book that had already been written, which is why I've also always had 'the sight'. I think probably most women have this, once they become aware of it, but I was aware of it from a young age. Ever since I nearly drowned and knew somehow beforehand that it was about to happen. As if someone was trying to warn me. I know now that that someone was me.

We've always had a strong connection; me, the mother, and the virgin. It means I have always felt at home hanging out with kids and with mothers, even when I was a middle-aged woman with no children. The people I hung out with from these different groups acted like I was one of them regardless. Because in an archetypal way, I was, and I still am. But all that aside, as the Crone, I am the embodiment of wisdom and achievement.

Ah, I have lived well... And have fulfilled on my ultimate dream, which was to live a passionate, compassionate and extraordinary life. I did all that, and now have the finishing line firmly in my sight. But I'm in no rush. I've got a few years left in me yet, and I intend to enjoy these with a little sit down at a tearoom, over a nice cream tea, and enjoy the view, before going through those big old red velvet curtains in the sky, where I will make my way on to the next place…

Right here and now, though, I'm in heaven.

DAWN

They were all sat in silence. It had taken them a little while to think upon it, but they had all noticed now that it was starting to get light outside. Still none of them wanted to say anything about it, though Marjorie had seen their fear was mounting.

"Where didst thou go?" asked the young girl.

Marjorie looked to Alice for clarity as she was not sure of the girl's meaning.

"When?" Marjorie asked.

"When thou didst ran away," she reminded her.

"Ah..." Marjorie said, catching up, "well, everywhere and nowhere. Back then, I were visible of course. Some would say too visible..."

"Too visible?" asked Alice, rubbing her leg. It had turned black and blue over the course of the night and had swollen up to twice the size. It desperately needed a poultice and Marjorie wished she had some herbs with her that could ease her suffering.

"Aye," she explained, "well there were them that did say I was quite a beauty."

Both women flicked glances at each and, though the room was murky, Marjorie saw that they were smirking at her,

"I'll thank thee not to look at me like that young mistresses!" she scolded.

They all laughed, and it felt good to be laughing still; though the laughs were sounding increasingly hollow.

"And didst thou never wish for childer?" asked the young one.

"Nay, bearing childer is a con."

Alice looked up at her shocked; her mouth dropping open.

"Well tis." Marjorie insisted, "a great big con to chain us mistresses to the bed and hearth. Because they know all too well that if we were out and about in the world, we would be poking our noses into their business in no time and showing them how it all needs doing. They canst be having that now can they; so they keep us busy."

She looked between the two women who were staring at her with wide eyes, both gawking. She realised that she had fallen in love with them both, just a little, over the course of the night. *Blasted Beltane, working your magic…* Marjorie cursed the spring. And then she began to open her heart…

"I never dreamt of getting married, but I dreamt of having childer. A huge brood…Mayhap eight or nine… But then, sometime after I had run away from home, mayhap aged twenty summers, I joined the church and became a wife of God, so had to put all dreams of child bearing to bed, and besides, there were orphans to look after, who had been left with me and the other sisters to take care of. But then the King's men came and threw us all out. When I turned forty summers… I had no husband. No childer. No house. No horse. No cart. Just the clothes on my back, and they were in tatters. I had my skills and my cunning and a lot of fine stories to tell… But folks care not about all that so much…

One Mistress, whose daughter I had birthed, invited me every year to the celebration of this child's life. On the 5th birthing day celebrations, on my way into the cottage, I met a young mistress with a toddling one and a newborn babe in a basket, struggling to get through the front gate. I went to help her, and she said to me, 'what are you doing here? There be no need for a midwife, and you have no childer.' And it made me feel… Well… And once this same child, unsure of my place within the world, said 'oh, you must be the spare mother' which made me laugh, but… it also made me feel like I had no place because I could not call myself a mother, or a wife. No one owned me… But I belonged to no-one either… Yet, I started to believe that I had no use… That I be no-one.

And I knew what was coming… For I knew about the change and there was no turning back… It felt like the end of something… But when it happened… And I became invisible… I also became free… It were not all well, of course… But it was not the end of the world neither. In fact, it felt like a new beginning. I could see clearly that all those trappings folk said I needed… That I thought I needed… To be someone… To be a mistress of importance… Well they were just yarns… We have all been spun bleedin yarns. And I know now that I just have to turn up to the day… And here I am…"

Marjorie turned to both the women and waved at them,

"Good Day!"

They both laughed and waved back enthusiastically.

"And that be enough…" she went on, "I be enough."

∞

Alice had never considered the possibility of embracing a life without childer. Every inch of her body inside and out had ached for a babe for a score more years. She had planned their names and had sewn their clothes. At first openly in front of John, but he grew sick of seeing them and scolded her, so then secretly when he did not come home from the ale house; pouring her hopes into the success of their unions. Praying, hoping, wishing and begging. Once she had been unable to take the pain in her heart any longer. She had run from the house one night after John had returned from the alehouse, well within his cups, and they had quarrelled, and he had called her barren. She had run out the door and through the gate, turning towards the church out of habit, but then found herself running past it towards the Long Man of Winelton Hill. With tears streaming down her face she had scrambled up the steep banks and crawled over the Longman, thumping her fists into his chest and face, as if he were John himself, and had screamed and wailed into the wind. Luckily it were the usual south easterly wind and so her curses had not carried towards the village. By the time she had returned to the cottage, mud smeared, and hair strewn, she found that John had passed out with his feet in the fire. She had left him there, having combed the embers away from him so they would not burn him, but so it would still look to him the next morning that he had narrowly escaped killing himself and setting fire to his whole house and his good wife in the process; hoping he would feel bad about his drinking. She had chuckled to herself, as it reminded her of the common jest, and as she climbed the narrow staircase to their bedchamber, she muttered to herself the punch line…

"He is the Master of the House, so he may sleep wherever he likes."

She muttered the line to herself again now and reflected on how it had not taught him a lesson. He had gone to the ale house again the night after still and most nights thereafter.

∞

Kitty looked up at the window. She had never thought on childer. Her life thus far had felt like one long fire fight and there had been little time for her to think on feelings such as maternal stirrings. She felt protective of her sisters, despite their disdain and coldness towards her, because she had seen enough of the world to know what awaited them outside their father's walls. How he would not protect them or consider their safety or comfort. And now it looked as if she would never have childer anyway. Upon the morrow she would either die, or somehow manage to secure her escape and would hence forth be a fellow. The thought of this drew blood to her chest. She desperately wanted to be free of her corset and coif. To be riding astride a stallion in breeches and for all the world to look upon her as a man.

To be a man. To be received as a man. It made her feel strong. Like she could even make this foolish plan work; it seemed like desperate madness. But the only way she could see to make it work, was if she did not think like a maid at all.

∞

Marjorie bent her head down and began to pray to herself once more. It seemed there was nothing more left to say. The light was growing bright now, which meant the sun was lurking just behind the forest and would soon burst forth through the church windows.

"Hail Mary full of Grace," Marjorie whispered quietly to herself. "The Lord is with thee. Blessed are thou amongst women and blessed is the fruit of thy womb, Jesus. Holy Mary, Mother of God, pray for us sinners now and at the hour of our death, Amen… Hail Mary full of Grace, the Lord is with thee. Blessed are thou amongst women and blessed is the fruit of thy womb, Jesus. Holy Mary, Mother of God, pray for us sinners now and at the hour of our death, Amen."

∞

Peering out the great window, Kitty could clearly see the detail again of the great twisting yew tree. In the dark shadows she had grown to despise the tree, but now she saw it again in the light, its spreading needle boughs that wove up from the graveyard like a hundred escaping souls, she found she could not feel resentment towards it. She had been climbing in it since she was a little girl. She knew every branch, every nook and cranny. It held her and kept her safe when she had needed to escape from the priest. It was her kith. It had not been the tree's fault that the men had been intent on trapping her. They had not even been intent on trapping all three of them. She had just been in the wrong place at the wrong time. They had only been after the old one, and that was only because she challenged them. For the men, it was a kind of luck that they also bagged two other troublesome mistresses in their quarrel. Kitty looked up at the tree; a flock of long tailed tits swooped down and caught upon it, as if the tree had snatched them from the air. Kitty loved Long Tailed Tits. They were her favourite bird. Along with wrens. She did love wrens. Their little round puffed up bodies. They were brave, though they be small. Kitty felt the strength now of a wren in her belly and she began to gently sing to herself;

"On the moor I saw a plover,
And a curlew called him lover,
Peewit!
Peewit!
Spring will surely come again."

She sang the tune through twice, quietly, when suddenly the plump one began to join in too. Turning, Kitty found the woman was hobbling over to her. She did not look well. She did not stand a chance of escaping.

∞

Looking across at how the colours were glowing again in the two remaining stained glass windows, Alice knew their time was growing short. The maid began to sing. It was a song her own mother had sung it to her when she had been a babe. Suddenly she needed to hold the girl again, and despite her leg, she rose up and made her way over to her. She needed to feel her warmth once more; before all warmth was taken from them. Alice joined the girl and wrapped her arms tightly around her, from behind, pulling her close into her embrace. They both looked up at the yew tree through the window, at the birds that fluttered around in its branches, and began to weep together as they sang their sweet, sweet song.

∞

Whilst their backs were turned, Marjorie reached into her basket. She had one small vial of hemlock. There was only enough for one person. She had been carrying this around for a long time, so it might not even be strong enough for one. Each of the Sisters were given a vial at the convent when the King's men had been sent upon the road to destroy them. Most of the Sisters had been virgins and would have rather taken their lives than have the men force themselves upon them. Many of them had drunk their vials. But Marjorie had not come to the convent a virgin, even before having spent many years under the roof of Mother Margaret. She had already had her fair share of men forcing themselves on her, and would not waste a vial of hemlock, or her own life for that matter, over a short bit of huffing and puffing from a worthless little man. She had not foreseen that this would be how and why she would have use of the hemlock, but she was glad to have it still. Pouring it within the last of the wine, she swivelled the powder around so that the tincture was lost in its depths.

Then she called to Alice and showed her that she should finish the last of the wine, and Alice hobbled over. She took the goblet and sipped upon it, but then she went to give the young maid the rest. Marjorie reached out and grabbed her cuff, pulling her back down onto the bench. At first the Mistress could not understand why she had been pulled back, but as Marjorie persisted to tap the bottom of the goblet, with knowing eyes, insisting that Alice drank it down, Alice began to dawn that the time had come to 'make it short'.

∞

Alice looked down at her reflection in the wine. She had never felt so brave or so alive. Everything was clear and crisp. She could hear all the birds in the yew tree. She could even smell the thick wood of the tree, through the stench of the straw on the floor, and despite the thick stone walls that enclosed them. She could feel the cloth of her smock against her skin. She could feel her empty womb. She took a deep breath... And drank down the wine.

As she lowered the goblet Marjorie called to the maid, who turned and looked at them; dropping her singing as she saw the look on Alice's face. Her eyes cast down to the goblet in Alice's hand and she watched as Alice began to squirm; the wine displeasing her innards and her breath beginning to tighten. The cunning woman indicated something to the girl and then she was pulling something out from her bodice, revealing a cloth tucked down deep inside. At first, she hesitated to show Alice, but as Alice writhed more, the girl could see she had not much time, and so opened out the cloth and showed Alice it contained some diamonds. Seeing the stones glistening in the morning light, Alice looked up into the girl's face, her heart brimming with joy. She was so grateful. She loved her. And wanted her to be safe. The maid grabbed her and sat down by her side, pulling hold of her on the bench, wrapping her arms around the woman. She was wriggling in pain as the poison ran through her body. She could not breathe. Her throat would not open. The maid began to sing again, trying to soothe her. And Alice tried to join in, but just made a rasping noise. On the other side of her the older woman was praying once more, looking up at the window. Foam began dropping from Alice's lips and with a last few convulsions, she went limp. The last thought in her mind, as she left her body, was that she never found out the young maid's name.

∞

The old woman finished her prayer with an 'Amen' as the woman's body slouched heavily in Kitty's arms. A sob burst from her mouth, but at that moment a loud bang came from the door and the sound of many angry voices. Kitty heard her father's voice, indignant with rage.

The old woman looked to Kitty and told her with a furious hiss…

"Whatever happens, act pious. Act stupid. Show me no mercy," she grabbed Kitty's face hard in her hand and pulled it towards hers, looking deep into her eyes "show me no mercy!" and Kitty was forced to nod furiously as she could not speak for the terror.

The old woman rose, then turned back briefly and cupped Kitty's face once more and kissed her forehead and whispered, "be brave!"

Kitty smiled briefly, but Marjorie had already hurled herself to the door, flying into a fit of rage; cursing and screeching like a mad woman.

Wikipedia – The Witch of Wineltone

Marjorie Brooks of Wineltone, Sussex, now known as Wilmington, was accused of witchcraft in the year 1550. Charged with murdering her neighbour, Mistress Anne Hathaway, and for poisoning another neighbour, Mistress Abys Day, who survived, but had *been possessed by a demon.*

Brooks was arrested along with two other women, but by the time the magistrate arrived, one of the women, a Mistress Alice Blackwater, was found to be dead, also through poisoning and a younger woman, whose name is not on record, was said to have been hysterical *as if possessed by some demon.* She was not charged, and Alice's name was cleared posthumously. Strangely, the unnamed younger woman vanished later that day, leaving no trace. Marjorie was accused of her vanishing.

Brooks was charged on the 3rd May 1550 on three counts of poisoning, two counts of murder, two counts of causing possession by demons and one count of vanishing. All committed through witchcraft. Marjorie pleaded guilty and was taken to the town of

Brighthelmstone where she was hanged on the 4th May 1550.

Accounts say she had been tortured so badly that two men had to hold her up to place her neck in the noose. She went to the gallows in deadly silence, as scolding water had been poured into her mouth, so she could not *bewitch any other.*

The sun rises over the hill and floods the carriage with sunlight. The men in the neighbouring carriage have finally drunk themselves into slumber, but Juliette and I have not felt safe enough to sleep. They have been in a few more times to use the toilet, being equally gross and lecherous every time, but the especially awful one has not reappeared. I guess perhaps there was another toilet in the other direction...

The young girl has been dosing for a few hours now and keeps talking in her sleep. She still has her earphones in and her head is leaning against the window. My phone died hours ago. I was on the phone to my husband, letting him know we'd be here for the night. The last announcement told us that there had been some damage done to the lines, this was just being fixed and apparently some arrests had been made. I can't believe it's dawn and we've been here all night. It is beautiful though. The golden light is full of brilliance.

"We've just watched the dawn after Beltane!" I say out loud, jolting Juliette slightly.

"Oh yes," she replies. "And we watched the sunset too..."

"We did..." I smile. "I can't remember the last time that happened, and I don't think I've ever done it sober. Not that I am sober, but you know what I mean."

Suddenly, the young girl jolts upright, taking in a huge gasp of air, as if she has been underwater. It makes us both jump and we turn to look at her, almost going to her, as if something is wrong. She looks at us blinking, not sure where she is. Then the recognition of our faces and the situation we are in begins to smooth across her furrowed brow.

"Nightmare?" asks Juliette. The girl blinks hard and looks out the window; face first into the brilliant morning light. She closes her eyes hard against it and drinks in the sun through her skin.

"I just dreamt I..." then she tails off and looks down at her hands. She looks like she is trying to find the words. She looks vulnerable suddenly. Less... Tough.

"Go on..." Juliette urges, "what were you dreaming?"

"You're not meant to talk about dreams," the girl murmurs. "It's boring."

Juliette laughs. Really laughs. A proper belly filled cackle.

"Boring for who?" she guffaws. There really is no other word for it. "The subconscious always gets our attention in the end. What's your interior world been telling you?"

The girl blinks and looks at us both, then back at her hands; pondering this for a moment. Her nails are bitten so short they look uncomfortably sore.

"I've been taking magic mushrooms," she says, so matter-of-factly I can hardly believe she just said it, "so I think it was more of a vision than a dream..."

∞

"Well now you've seriously piqued my interest," I say smirking and turning my full body and attention towards her, slapping my hands down on my thighs and rubbing them in excitement, "go on then. If you're going to take mushrooms all night, without offering us any, then I demand to know what visions you've been summoning up. I expect you've been listening to us chatting as well, haven't you?"

The girl goes red and shuffles uncomfortably in her seat.

"You know all our secrets then," I continue, "and I expect any visions you've had are partly thanks to our titillating conversations and wit. So, come on then... Let's be having you."

The girl takes in a deep breath and turns to face us, the sun shines brightly around the sides of her head, creating a halo effect.

"I dreamt that I was in a jungle and someone gave me a strong hallucinogenic drink. The guy who gave it to me was a... erm..."

"A shaman?" I suggest.

"Yes. He was the village shaman. Well, then suddenly we were in a large red and yellow big top tent... But still in the jungle... You two were there too..."

"Oh lovely," I encourage, "I've always wanted to go to the jungle."

The girl laughs and sees I'm not mocking her but am genuinely interested. She grows in confidence.

"A powerful looking punk woman had built the tent for the shaman as a gift because the shaman had cured her of cancer. There was a sign outside that had the shaman's face on it, surrounded by jaguars, all wearing big red noses, and underneath it the sign read: *The Circus of the Jaguar Blood*. I went inside and it felt a bit like a church. I thought to myself *this is my kind of church!"*

"Sounds fabulous," I encourage her.

"I didn't know him, but the shaman welcomed me in like an old friend, like we knew each other really well or something, and then the ceremony began. He said he was dedicating the ceremony to Mother Earth. He told us that she was in pain. He told us that all the women with us in the tent, and all the women on the planet, are like, versions of Mother Earth, which I understood as it meant we're all different aspects of her."

"That's right" I say. "We are all facets of the divine feminine. Like the different edges of a cut jewel. We are all individual, but all part of one whole inner divine jewel."

The girl looks at me for a long moment, as if she is seeing me for the first time. Young people always think us oldies are so dull.

"Exactly," she eventually nods and agrees.

"He said," the girl goes on, "the ceremony will be in worship of Mother Earth and in worship of all of us. All the women in the tent and the aspects we represent…"

"Archetypes?" I suggest.

"I guess so," agrees the girl smiling, knowing I'm referring to my previous conversation with Esme; the blonde woman opposite me.

∞

Looking at the girl, I begin to beam with excitement. It feels so good to hear her speaking properly.

"Then some people wafted smoke over each of us like it was a blessing, like a cleansing thing. And then the shaman blessed the drink we were drinking. We took it in turns to go up and drink. As I drank the stuff, I thought it tasted like mud, and I was gonna be sick; but I didn't throw up. Then I returned to my mat at the edge of the tent and got under a blanket…"

She looks up at us, to see if we are listening, and sees me smiling. She gives me the cutest little smirk of pleasure. The sun is so bright behind her, that her halo grows bigger and wider. I wonder how old she is… nineteen, maybe twenty years old? My breath catches suddenly as I consider the fact that I am old enough to be her mother!

"Have you ever been worshipped before?" she asks us suddenly. Juliette turns and looks at me thoughtfully, trying to recall if she has… I sure as hell know I haven't. I start to shake my head…

"No" I respond.

∞

The old woman screws up her eyes, thinking, and then shakes her head too.

"Me neither, obviously." I say, sharing my mad, mushroom infused dream with two complete strangers on a train that I've been stranded on ALL FUCKING NIGHT. I wish I'd bothered to speak to them earlier now. Could have had some wine.

"Well, I realised, that was exactly what I was feeling in the dream, that the overall feeling was that I was being worshipped. And it felt like pure love. Like I kind of stepped out of the dream for a moment and thought *this is what pure love feels like.* Whatever I had drunk was teaching me whatever I needed to know, but everything it was doing, it was doing it from a place of pure love. And so, I was being worshipped as a divine feminine being… And it was… Well…"

For some reason the memory makes me start to laugh. I look up at them, feeling so fucking embarrassed to be talking like this at them, to these… Strangers. But I'm met by two sets of bright sparkling eyes. And my heart feels so filled up with joy…

"Well," I carry on, feeling stronger than I've ever felt, "the shaman started singing. He sang words I didn't know, but it seemed as if they were about worshipping the earth and all the women in the tent. And as he sung, I sort of turned into a snake. But I also felt like I was having sex. Not with anyone or anything. I was feeling like I was having sex without anyone touching me. It was all coming from inside me, like I was sex, and I could feel everyone else in the tent was also feeling something similar. Like I had octopus tentacles or something and they were reaching out and touching the people lying next to me, whether I liked it or not. And I was affecting their visions and, I guess, turning them on.

And then, the shaman sang into the back of his drum, really loudly, and it blew my mind. It sounded like, like a kind of voice of a caveman or something... As if it was from the back of a cave, from like, the old days... When we were cavemen. And then you two and everyone else in the tent turned into women sitting in a big circle together. We were dressed in old clothes and passing a golden nut to each other. I think it was a hazelnut, but it might have been a walnut. Then when the nut finished being passed around the circle, I saw a golden beam of light blast down the centre of the tent and fan out in rays; each one hitting each of the women in the circle. We all sort of blew up. All our bodies blew up in a cloud of dust as some bigger thing made of bright golden light blew out from inside of us and we each became these great big larvae type things made of bright golden light. I realised we were all queen bees and our bodies were pulsating, like we were constantly having sex and pushing out babies." I laugh at myself then, realising how fucking barking I sound. "I don't know if you know about that?" I ask them, turning towards the two women, trying to show them I don't need locking up. "That queens bees look like maggoty things and they're always pushing out babies? Like all day long and forever and ever?"

"That's right," the old woman agrees with me. "They're always fucking."

This makes me laugh. For some reason, it's always funny to hear old people swear.

"Yeah, I saw it on Attenborough recently…" the middle-aged woman says.

"That's right," I agree eagerly, "that's where I saw it too and I guess that's what made me think of it. I became this one big, like, non-stop orgasm."

They both laugh when I say this, and I crack up too. How mad is that?

"I gave in to it, to the sex and pleasure of it all, and suddenly for the first time in my life, I felt like, HER… Like a she. But not just any she, I felt like Mother Earth. Whoever or whatever that is… Well, like, as if she was in the tent with us. She was behind me, in me, was part of me. I've never felt anything like it before. I could really feel her. That SHE was part of me.

"Like an archetype?" Suggested the old woman again.

"Yes!" I laugh. I get what she is going on about now. "Like, a puppet playing her on earth, with HER close to my shoulders, behind my back, guiding me; like a puppet master. Or mistress, I guess. Like SHE was my mother and I was also my own mother. Does that make any sense?"

"Sort of," they both agree.

∞

Just hearing this makes my skin prickle. I can see HER now here, in the golden sun that is shining behind our young friend. In all the beautiful countryside that pours out into the distance beyond the train. The Goddess is here with us. Always. I also feel her in me. And I suddenly feel invincible. Then I notice a sense that there are more than three of us in the carriage. A play of the light perhaps? But it looks, no, *feels*, as if there are shadows with us, between us. Like six of us are sat together.

"Then the world fell away into a whole load of different images. I can't recall all of them now, but I remember, at one point, I was a little kid being pinned down by a puppy that was licking my face and it was the funniest thing ever. I screamed and squealed. Then that vision finished, and I said *thank you* and a neon sign appeared of a little Japanese girl's cartoon face and a speech bubble coming out of her mouth saying, *you're welcome!*

Then I had another vision where there was a web, like a spider's web, that was woven around the Earth, and it was covered in dew drops. Some of these dew drops were lighting up gold and as they did so, the light was travelling through the web until it reached the next dew drop, and then those ones lit up too. The light was spreading across the surface of the planet…"

"Tom saw that!" Juliette interrupts, "on his death bed. A day or two before he died… He said he could see a web that wrapped around the world. Like a kind of energy."

"I've seen something like this too…" I suddenly recall, realising the last time I was on LSD, many years ago, I had seen a similar vision. "It was a layer that floated about half a meter above the floor, about ten centimetres thick, made up of thousands of iridescent worms, all writhing around each other. I saw it as being the energy of the earth…"

"Yes!" shouts the young person, excited to know she is not alone, "and then I understood that this was a worldwide women's web, like the internet, and each dew drop was a different woman. I saw that the web was made of a rope, like an umbilical cord, or a double helix; twisting the different generations together. And as different women wake up, they inspire the women around them to wake up too and that's what was making them start to glow gold."

"My favourite friends are women outside of my age group." I interject, "It feels like there is no competition between us. Like we can help each other out, even if we're similar, because we're not in danger of stepping on each other's toes."

"Huh" muses Juliette. I guess she's never thought of that before and I feel chuffed to have shared some wisdom with her.

"Did you know that when women are born," I carry on, feeling fortified, "they already hold inside themselves all the eggs they'll bleed throughout their lives, and any eggs that will become fertilised and turn into babies. Which means all of us, in egg form, were once in our grandmother's wombs."

"Bleugh!" the young one pretends to puke, mock putting her fingers in her mouth.

"I'm afraid I have to agree with you there!" laughs Juliette. "Can't think of anything more awful."

"Although, that's what I was seeing…" the young one replies, checking back in with herself. "The web that was lighting up, was showing me that Mother Earth is waking up. She had been sent away by like… men, I guess… ages ago, but she has just been sleeping. Now she is waking up and is on her way downstairs… And she is going to be pissed when she sees the mess we've made. And it means the women on earth are waking up too. And the men who care, who are not afraid of Mother Earth; they are waking up too. The worldwide web of women is waking up. And it is through women and men who give a shit, that she will get us to clear the place up, before it's too late. Before we all kill ourselves. Because that's what we need to do, isn't it? We need to clear up the fucking mess..."

The light is almost blinding me now and the double vision is growing stronger. Each of us women are shedding second silhouettes beside us, I can only see them out of the corners of my eyes, if I don't look directly at them. I think they are silhouettes, but I swear the one beside me is wearing an apron.

∞

I'm wonderfully taken by this incandescent being who is glowing now, not just from the sun, but also with joy. And her words are inviting others in. I think Esme has noticed them too. Others are here with us.

"Yes," I agree, "We don't need a knight in shining armour to ride in and save us. One man, riding into the rescue... He will be too easy to cut down. We need loving and caring people from all over the world to all work together. Then we can't be taken out."

"Exactly," continues the young visionary; "the ones who are making all the mess.

They're not expecting us to work together..."

"They're used to hierarchy..." I interject.

"But this ain't that," our friend continues, "This is...?"

"Community," I smile.

Esme has tears on her cheeks, and I feel them pricking my eyes too. I reach out and take Esme's hand and she reaches out towards the young one, who comes over to our seats and sits beside me; taking both our hands and squeezing them tightly. Three strangers. All beautiful beings who feel like soul mates.

"I've never believed in the idea of Sisterhood," I laugh, holding on tightly to the two hands. "I've never felt it. And I've never trusted other women. My mother put pay to that. But you're right. Something is stirring. Even if we don't agree with each other, or even understand each other, we need to stop pointing the finger and instead, have each other's backs..."

∞

I am crying. I am tired and hungry, and listening to this vision has overwhelmed me.

I haven't really thought about the size of the situation we all currently find ourselves in, with climate change and all the rest of the shit that's going on in the world, and I realise how utterly powerless I've been feeling. And that I'm trying to force, literally force, a child into the world, knowing what that child faces. But hearing this young person… well, I feel hope.

Hope that I didn't even know I needed. I take a deep breath and try to pull myself together. I look up and see that Juliette is welling up too and as our eyes meet, she reaches out and pulls me into her arms. Then she pulls the young one into her arms too and we're all suddenly hugging each other, sobbing uncontrollably.

∞

I can't believe I'm hugging two strangers. I feel so stupid, but I also have never felt happier. I'm clearly still tripping balls…

The train jolts.

"This is your conductor speaking, the trees have all been cleared and the tracks have been repaired. We will shortly be on our way. The service will be returning to

Brighton and not continuing to Ashcroft International as previously scheduled. Repeat; this service will be returning to Brighton and not carrying on to Ashcroft International as previously scheduled. We apologise for all the inconvenience that this has caused."

We whoop in excitement and begin to gather our possessions. I pack up my phone and earbuds, then see the half-eaten bag of mushrooms at the bottom of my rucksack.

"Fancy one then?"

The women both laugh at me.

"I'm okay for mushrooms, thank you," says the older one, "But have you got anything to smoke?"

I smirk at her. She *does* know the smell then.

As the train starts to haul itself back the way we came, the men in the next carriage start to stir, much less noisy than earlier and sounding well hungover. We all laugh at them. In the golden light of dawn, they suddenly seem a lot less scary.

The train slides its way like a snake through the curvy folds of the South Downs, making its way back towards the city, bathed in the brilliant light of a brand new day.

A NEW DAY

Sat around the back of the station, on the benches in front of a yet to open café, I pass back and forth a one skin spliff with the older woman, Juliette. She has reapplied her bright red lipstick and is leaving a raunchy rouge tip on the roach. Taking in an impressive toke, she passes it to me and says:

"Well, surmountable at least..." she is talking about men, or the patriarchy, as she's calling it.

"It's weird, because I've never liked girls," I explain, "I mean, I fancy them, but all my friends are men. All the girls at school were total bitches, and I didn't meet any women I liked to hang out with until I moved to Brighton."

"I think Brighton attracts the kind of women who only ever hung out with boys at school," muses the middle aged one, Esme, who says no to the spliff. "All my mates here used to be tom boys."

"I'd love to have been born a man" sighs Juliette as she takes back the spliff and sucks down another deep toke.

"It would be amazing to be male," Esme agrees. "I wouldn't be injecting myself in the stomach every day and going for operations to have my eggs sucked out if I had a penis. All my husband has had to do through this whole IVF nightmare is wank in a cup. It's so fucking unfair."

"Things are going to get a whole lot worse before they get any better," considers Juliette. "You know I met a chap the other day who is an entrepreneur and an investment banker. He was telling me all about his vision of the future. I said to him, you know all the trees are dying, don't you? They're giving up. And without trees we will all die. You know what he said to me? That mankind will invent something that will replace trees. Automated trees. And they'd be even more efficient. The world is utterly deluded. We don't deserve to be here. And I, for one, am glad I won't be around much longer."

"Is there any hope then?" Esme asks Juliette.

"Yes!" I answer, my voice erupting suddenly from somewhere deep in my gut, "if we're brave and all work together… And if we take more mushrooms."

They all laugh.

Flicking the roach into the air, I grab my bag and make my farewells. I really need a piss. We all say goodbye and the women walk away in the opposite direction to me, through the bright spring light; back towards their lives. I head off with my shadow stretching out in front of me, feeling fortified by having met them both. My heart feels full, with a whole new kind of love.

∞

Mother Earth blows them all a kiss on the breeze, wishing them good luck and willing them to do well. Smiling, she turns with a chuckle and returns to cavorting with her sexy new sun, who is still dressed in his current favourite green man harlequin outfit. Clicking his heel three times in the air, they skip off together over the downs to the sound of shimmering bells.

A red admiral flutters past.

And a wren pops out to pick at the roach butt, but decides it is not an early worm, so darts off in search of something juicer.

FOR SISTERS EVERYWHERE;

- Connect with the other generations.
- Trust in your fellow sisters.
- Trust yourself.
- Take courage and stand up for what you believe in.
- Together we will steer this world into safer waters.
- Let the divine feminine, the cyclical and our connection to Mother Nature, back into our lives.
- Remember… You are divine. You are a sacred space.
- Know that you are part of a lineage.
- Know that this planet does need saving and we are the ones to save it.
- But men are not the enemy. Toxic masculinity and patriarchy are they problem and they are fucking things up for everyone.

WE'VE GOT THIS

Printed in Poland
by Amazon Fulfillment
Poland Sp. z o.o., Wrocław

52776222R00176